ᛏ

ᚨ.ᚾ.

Alex got ou...
fell asleep

and walked out onto the balcony. He leaned on the railing, staring unseeingly at the ocean. He lit a cigarette, then tossed it away, furious at himself. Feeling anything for his ex-wife had not been part of his plan.

He had to be single-minded about nailing Cruzero, who was nothing more than a sleazy, slippery drug trafficker. But fortunately or unfortunately for Alex, Sara wouldn't believe Cruzero was anything more than her wonderful old friend. Alex was sure he was just using Sara to get Cruzero. He couldn't let any feelings for a woman who'd walked out on him get in the way of his ultimate goal. But as he turned to look at Sara's sleeping form, where she lay exhausted by his lovemaking, he had to admit she still had a dangerous hold on him. . . .

Dear Reader,

The New Year is starting off splendidly here at Silhouette Intimate Moments. Take our American Hero, for instance. Riley Cooper, in Marilyn Pappano's *No Retreat,* is a soldier with a soft side. When his first love walks back into his life, troublemaking son in tow, it's surrender time for this tough guy.

Laurey Bright, long a favorite with readers of the Silhouette Special Edition line, makes her first Intimate Moments novel a winner. In *Summers Past* you'll find passion, betrayal and one all-important question: Who *is* little Carley's father? Allyson Ryan's *Secrets of Magnolia House* takes a few spooky detours along the road to romance; I think you'll enjoy the ride. *Two for the Road* is the first of Mary Anne Wilson's new "Sister, Sister" duo; look for *Two Against the World,* coming soon. Joanna Marks lights up the night with *Heat of the Moment*, and Justine Davis checks in with *Race Against Time,* a tale full of secrets, crackerjack suspense and irresistible desire. In short—I don't think you'll want to miss a single one of this month's books.

As the year goes on, look for books by more of your favorite authors. Kathleen Eagle, Doreen Roberts, Paula Detmer Riggs and Marilyn Pappano are only a few of the great writers who'll be coming your way in Silhouette Intimate Moments. And then there's our Tenth Anniversary celebration in May! Be sure to join us for all the fun.

Leslie Wainger
Senior Editor and Editorial Coordinator

HEAT
OF
THE
MOMENT

Joanna
Marks

Silhouette® V™
INTIMATE MOMENTS®
Published by Silhouette Books New York
America's Publisher of Contemporary Romance

SILHOUETTE BOOKS
300 East 42nd St., New York, N.Y. 10017

HEAT OF THE MOMENT

Copyright © 1993 by Jo Ann Darby

ISBN: 0-373-07473-5

First Silhouette Books printing January 1993

All the characters in this book have no existence outside the imagination of the author and have no relation whatsoever to anyone bearing the same name or names. They are not even distantly inspired by any individual known or unknown to the author, and all incidents are pure invention.

Printed in the U.S.A.

Books by Joanna Marks

Silhouette Intimate Moments

Love is a Long Shot #315
Wild at Heart #443
Heat of the Moment #473

JOANNA MARKS

didn't realize it at the time, but she prepared early to be a novelist. In the second grade, according to her teacher, she entertained her class with her stories. She's still concocting stories, now romances. She has spent time in England, Libya and Colombia, and currently lives in Florida.

Prologue

Afternoon sunlight streamed into the hospital room several floors up from the heavy traffic in the streets of downtown Miami. The television set, above the bed, pumped out the midday news. A panel of buttons at easy reach allowed Sara, propped up in the bed, to reach out and change the channel. The picture on the screen flipped over to another program—a talk show with an audience shouting and laughing at some comment the host had just made, but it didn't hold Sara's interest.

Her restless gaze swung to the hallway. A nurse hovered in front of a medical cart with rows of drawers. Each drawer held medication the nurse doled out with methodical care to patients in rooms lining both sides of the obstetrics unit.

For a few moments Sara sat watching her, yet not really seeing her, her mind filled with other thoughts.

With a halfhearted intention of making an inspection
of her appearance, Sara picked up the tortoiseshell
compact from the nightstand and popped it open as
she lifted it to see her image. Luminous gray eyes that
seemed to be searching for something and a well-
formed mouth full of sensual promise met her scrutiny. Her face was pale without any trace of makeup.
A wealth of blond hair in tangled chaotic curl.

"You look like something the cat dragged in," she
observed softly. But there was no desire to alter that
impression, no enthusiasm to do anything about it.
She snapped the compact shut.

She had lost the baby, she observed thoughtfully; it
had been the only thing holding her and Alex together. Nothing was going to keep them together now,
she was convinced of that. A tear slipped from her eye
and she rubbed it away quickly with the back of her
hand. Her head sank back into the pillow, her eyes
filled with resolve. She was getting out of here. There
was no point in sticking around. Their six-week marriage was a patchwork fiasco after a whirlwind affair
that had been marked from the start by unbridled
reckless passion. Another rogue tear slipped from her
other eye, and she furtively rubbed it away, then
blinked rapidly, just in time.

A man, tall, leanly muscled and powerfully built,
hovered in the doorway for a moment, openly assessing her. He had the darkly handsome features of a
matador or some other charismatic killer, but he wore
a business suit, crisp shirt and tie.

"How are you feeling, Sara?" He gave her name the
Spanish pronunciation.

"I'm fine." The injection of a casual lightness in her tone couldn't disguise the false note in her voice that she felt sure he detected immediately. Alex was one of the best narcotics detectives in the Miami Police Department; he was also one hip Cuban.

Instead of continuing the conversation after the initial greeting, he turned away. Remaining in the doorway, he stood talking to a nurse. Sara's husband of six weeks was an amalgam of Cuban roots and an American education. Cool on the outside when it came to his profession, he was pure Latin in his emotional makeup regarding women. With an inexhaustible supply of willpower and a passionate and volatile temperament, he tended to dominate women immediately with his sheer presence. Out of the corner of her eye Sara observed the nurse. Even the hard-boiled nurse looked a little overwhelmed. Most women were by Alex. They usually fell over themselves to assist him with whatever he wanted. He bombarded the nurse with a barrage of questions, but Sara caught only the last snatch of conversation.

"There is absolutely nothing to worry about, Mr. Cordera, I assure you. She's young, healthy, there's no reason why she can't have other children—those were the doctor's words exactly, not mine." The nurse turned back to the cart and the task of doling out medications, consulting her index file.

Sara pushed herself up against the pillows as Alex swung around and moved back into the room with a stealthy natural animal grace.

"The nurse says you're going to be okay," he said, smiling warmly at her.

"I'm definitely not going to die." She laughed softly and pushed her tumbling hair from the side of her face with a gesture that was almost blasé. "Miscarriages at three months are very common."

Alex watched every nuance of movement and expression. "I'm sorry I couldn't get here sooner, Sara. If I could have, I would have been here last night." His Cuban manner of speaking, a quick staccato roll to his words, rhythmic and slightly accented, was very engaging. When he was irritated he spoke so rapidly all the words ran together.

"I hardly ever see you since you were assigned to this special task force."

"I have a job to do, Sara. You know that. You believe me when I say I'm sorry I wasn't here?" Burnt sienna eyes bored into hers.

"I believe you. I know it wasn't your fault. There was nothing you could have done if you had been here," she responded perfunctorily, averting her gaze but not in time to miss the telltale muscle flex in his jaw. Her response didn't satisfy him.

"I wanted to be here with you. I hope you believe me also when I say I'm very sorry about the baby."

In the same perfunctory way she responded, "I believe you. Besides, it doesn't matter now." Her voice trailed off and she looked at him again. Like a lot of things she said or did, her reply only seemed to anger him. She could see his temper revving up; he was starting to do one of his characteristic slow burns.

"What do you mean it doesn't matter, Sara? It matters to me. Do you hear what I'm saying? I wanted to be here with you. I'm sorry we lost the baby. I

wanted you to have this baby. What about you? Did
you want this baby?''

For a long moment Sara assessed what he was saying. He was a man bent on doing the right thing, a
man who came from a background where children
were adored, treasured, where they were shown endless patience and tolerance. That was what was motivating him to say these things. Alex was doing what his
background dictated. She wasn't fooling herself.

"I wanted this baby, too," she said flatly, no emotion visible in her face.

More than you'll ever know, she felt like crying out.
The baby was the only thing holding us together. She
cried the words softly in her mind. She suppressed the
strong emotion threatening to choke off her voice,
clamping down on it so swiftly that it was instantly
hidden, swallowed up inside her.

She knew her attitude baffled her husband. Turning his head away to gaze momentarily at some distant point in space, he swore softly before dragging in
his breath. Simultaneously, impatient tanned fingers
slipped inside his suit jacket pocket for a cigarette that
he couldn't smoke in the hospital. Then he turned
back to face her.

"You know something, Sara, ever since we met we
had this language barrier between us—something that
prevents us from getting through to each other. Do
you think maybe it's some kind of cultural gap?''

The deceptively warm humor didn't disguise the
bitter irony behind his words. She knew any minute his
expression could change, flashing into volatile impatience. The comment was a veiled reference to the past.
When they had first met she had given him the im-

pression that she was older and more experienced than she actually was. Any reference to the past such as that one made Sara instantly clam up, putting her immediately on the defensive. Her silence only seemed to provoke Alex more.

"Is everything all right in here? Are they treating you okay?"

Resentful over his veiled remark, her temper flared back at him. "I thought you just discussed all that with the nurse while I sat here like some child."

"I wanted to make sure there were no complications."

"You could have asked me. I could have told you that. I'm nineteen—not mentally backward."

"Wow. So much sweetness in one woman. I'm a lucky guy," he said with amusement, but his mocking scrutiny only irritated her and unnerved her more.

"And don't look at me—I look a mess and I know it." She shoved a hand through her mop of blond hair, but it was an exercise in futility. Her hair fell back down to the side of her face.

"You look fine to me." He laughed with soft intimacy. "Why do women always think they have to look glamorous? Do they think men like all that junk they put on?"

"Yes," she said mutinously. "Because *most* of them do."

"I don't." His eyes drilled the message home.

"No," she taunted. "You like your women naked, submissive and—"

"Pregnant? Not if I can help it, Sara."

Her face flushed darkly as she averted her gaze. Her fingers pulled at the satin ribbon of the *broderie an-*

glaise nightgown she was wearing. That was a direct reference to the fact that she had let him think she was "experienced" and then had been totally unprepared. She didn't want to open up that can of worms, so she summed up her condition triumphantly.

"Well, I'm not pregnant anymore," she pointed out.

"You can have other children, Sara."

"Maybe I don't want any," she said defiantly, looking straight at him. "There's nothing for you to worry about now, because I'm not pregnant. I'm fine. I'm really fine."

"What's that suppose to mean? You're fine. I'm fine. Everything's fine, our whole relationship so far has been fine, except we never know what we're talking about. 'Cause there's only one place we really communicate." Lazy humor drifted across to her. "That's in bed."

"Since I never see you until it's good and dark, that's hardly a problem, is it?" she sniped back. When she looked up again Alex studied her with barely concealed impatience, waiting. He was having trouble controlling his young wife and he didn't like it much. Sara knew she was behaving abysmally but she couldn't help herself. When he was like this he drove her to it; she dug in her heels and fought him every inch of the way, locking all her feelings inside her. Alex had the look of a man who knew he should be saying something tender and understanding, considering what had just happened to them, turning on some of that Cuban charm he was so capable of. But she knew the way she was acting didn't encourage him to get started, and his own macho arrogance got in the way.

"You want to play games, Sara. Okay. We can play games." A hard edge crept into his voice and eyes. "How much longer do you have to stay in here?"

"Until tomorrow." She pushed herself up against the pillows again, and the nightgown strained against her full breasts. A very male look of possession followed the movement. When it left the neckline of the nightgown and reached her face, their eyes locked. The heat she felt fanning her skin and cheekbones in waves was mutual; she saw it reflected in his eyes. He made no effort to disguise it.

"I thought you would be discharged today." *He wanted her back* was the silent message behind the words.

"I don't mind staying another night."

Busy studying her with a street-smart look, he made no comment.

Sara inspected his broad shoulders and the virile way his thick hair grazed the collar of his crisp white shirt. Even on the job as a narcotics detective he was always immaculate, dressed to advantage, his dark good looks emphasized by a well-cut suit.

"Maybe you think it's nicer here than back there with me," he said, flashing one of his deceptively amiable smiles that concealed other thoughts.

"I never said that."

"Maybe you were thinking it, Sara. You never tell me what you're thinking, except when you're taking shots at me, so I'm never sure what's really going on inside that beautiful head of yours. Maybe that's part of the attraction." A smile curved his sensual mouth.

Bracing an arm on either side of her, his lips only inches from hers, he gave her a quick kiss. Then his

gaze swung to check the steel Rolex watch on his wrist
and he muttered a soft Spanish expletive. "Someone
is covering for me—that's the only reason I was able
to get away. I want to stay, but I have to go," he said
with a look of genuine regret. For a long moment he
stood over her as if reluctant to move. "Do you want
me to get you anything? Is there anything that you
need?"

"I don't need anything. Everything's fine. Really.
I'm..."

The deceptive, ever-present smile remained, but she
recognized the slow burn in his eyes. "I know, Sara.
You're fine. I'm fine. Everything's fine." The fiery
staccato explosion ceased.

A voice inside her head cried softly, *We don't stand
a chance now. It's all over. Can't you see that?* They
stared at each other in the sizzling silence.

"They're waiting for me downstairs. I'll be back
tomorrow." He reached down, his lean tanned fingers capturing the curve of her neck with telling
strength. His mouth claimed hers in a hungry, warm
kiss, fueled by the same raw attraction that had pulled
them together and caused all the trouble in the first
place, Sara thought breathlessly.

Straightening slowly, he looked down at her, then
grazed her chin playfully with his fist. "Don't flirt
with any of these young doctors around here." He indicated the hallway with a tilt of his head. "You got
it?"

For a moment the matador smile mesmerized her,
but she noticed his measuring look. As if he was satisfied with some inner conclusion, the look vanished
as quickly as it had arrived. With an air of self-

possession he turned and disappeared out the door. She heard him talking to the nurse in the hallway, firing words at her in a low staccato barrage.

Being married to a detective had its disadvantages. When he was around, Alex usually had all the angles figured out, with a tendency to be two jumps ahead of her. She hoped he didn't figure out this angle until she was safely on a plane to California.

Her heart was a throbbing drum, beaten by her own premeditated deception, because her mind was racing, plotting an escape from a relationship that was never meant to be. The passionate attraction they had felt for each other was like some hothouse plant forced into bloom under artificial conditions. Convinced it was only going to wither and die, Sara didn't feel like hanging around to watch the death throes of a relationship she was sure would end with them hating each other. There was the only way to deal with Alex, if all that formidable willpower was not to overwhelm her. He would try to stop her, for sure. But as she watched him disappear down the corridor—his familiar dark head, his proud bearing hinting at his magnetic personality—something in her died, too. She wanted to leap out of the bed and run after him, fling herself into his arms, mold her body against his and beg him never, never to let her go. But she clamped down on her strong heartfelt desires, much the way she had suppressed her responses when he asked if she wanted their baby—thinking she had mastered them, thinking she could control them and bury them forever.

As she leaned her head back into the soft pillows, the death of her parents chose that moment to come back into her mind. They had been involved in a head-on car crash, killed instantly. The absence of their loving warmth had left a huge gaping hole in her life, leaving her off balance emotionally, ready for some kind of intense relationship. She had a younger sister, but their age difference had loomed large at that point in their lives. She'd had friends, but nothing took the place of people who really loved and cared about you.

When she walked into that dark club with some of her wilder friends, without realizing it she had found what she was looking for. Macho, handsome, brimming over with Cuban charm and ten years older, Alex Cordera had her fascinated, flattered and deeply drawn to him from the first moment his eyes locked onto hers. Winding up the evening after a party, dressed in a provocative black dress, with a veneer of sophistication from living in foreign countries with her parents, she had let him think she was older and much more experienced than she was. At the time Sara had thought she was only looking for romance, a little excitement, a good time, when what she had been really looking for was love. She had no appreciation of the fire she played with or the strength of the emotions that gripped her or of how rapidly the situation would advance between them. She had been caught totally unprepared; so had Alex.

When he discovered her true age and that she was pregnant, Alex had taken charge of the situation immediately. He'd issued commands with brusque hammerlike precision about what they *were* and *weren't* going to do, and they had gotten married hastily. But after they were married he always seemed as though he was experiencing some kind of slow burn. Her own deepening sense of guilt put her continually on the

defensive. When he came back to their condo at night
they often clashed over nothing at all. It was as if there
was some constant raging contest going on between
them, a silent battle to see who was going to get the
upper hand. Alex wanted control, a kind of subtle
domination over his young wife that his Latin ego demanded, while Sara, in spite of their situation, was not
going to knuckle under to his macho arrogant postur-
ing, which only provoked his temperament all the
more.

Now there was no child, and as devastated as Sara
was, she felt in her heart it was wrong to take advantage of his desire to do the right thing. It was wrong to
make Alex go on paying for the rest of his life for a
mistake that she felt deep down was more hers than
his, and that had been egged on by circumstances in
her life. Passion, love, lust, infatuation? Who could
distinguish one from the other in the heat of the moment at nineteen?

With ground-eating stride, Alex made his way out
of the hospital. All his thoughts were centered on his
young wife. No one else in the world could get him
going the way she could—Sara was a piece of work, all
right. The news from the hospital last night that his
wife had suffered a miscarriage had brought a stab of
keen disappointment. Once he had gotten used to the
idea of becoming a father he had discovered he liked
it. That was after he got over the initial shock of
Sara's walking up to him in public with a look in her
eyes and the announcement that she was pregnant.

With a wry twist curving his mouth, he remembered how he had grabbed her, hustled her some-

where private and informed her that you didn't just walk up to a guy in broad daylight and tell him a thing like that. He knew he should have been more gentle with her back in that hospital room; he should have shown her more tenderness. But these days Sara brought out only his hardened macho instincts. He didn't want to show her the gentleness within him. He wanted to dominate her, not reveal his innermost feelings. The truth was he wasn't sure what they were.

Everything had happened so fast between them. He knew he wanted her; he had never had any doubts about that. From the moment he saw her walk into that club with her friends he had known that. He had sent her a signal and she had shot him a look that was unmistakable. He knew his way around women. He knew when a woman reciprocated what he was feeling. He had moved in quickly, not giving her much time to change her mind. Maybe she'd gotten more than she bargained for when he decided to go for it.

She was beautiful. Most of the time she acted older than nineteen, and for a while she'd had him fooled about her true age. In spite of her age Sara had a lot going for her. A gorgeous smile, intelligence and wit, and a body that would tempt any man who didn't have one foot in the grave. She also had a passionate nature that matched his own. That was their undoing. But women who were lukewarm had never appealed to him. Yet what had really gotten to him more than anything else, what had brought out his intense desire for sole possession, was that ''looking for love'' expression in her eyes. When he found out her age he knew he should have walked away. But by then he couldn't keep his hands off her. When he found out he

had made her pregnant, he knew there was only one
course of action for him to take. They were getting
married, and the sooner the better.

He squinted in the dazzling Florida sunlight, his
sharp gaze surveying the parking lot to locate his
partner. He had a job to do and there was no more
time to think about his personal life. He made himself a promise that he would try to put things right between him and Sara when he picked her up tomorrow.
He hailed the rookie detective who had driven him to
the hospital and was working with him. In moments
the car screeched to a halt at the hospital entrance-
way, and Alex slid inside.

Later that day Sara signed herself out of the hospital. She had to go now, before Alex came for her. She
took a taxi back to the condo, telling the driver to return for her in an hour.

Before leaving the condo she took a long, last lin-
gering look. Some deep emotion welled up inside her,
and for a moment she almost wavered. But then her
inner resolve brought her emotions to heel. A clean
break was the best thing for both of them, her inner
voice reasoned. It was never meant to be. Tearing a
piece of notepaper from a scratch pad, she scrawled a
hasty note.

> I'm leaving. I'm not coming back. It's never go-
> ing to work out between us. Sometimes things
> happen for the best.
>
> > Sara.

She slipped it into an envelope, sealed it and left it
on the kitchen snack bar where he was sure to find it

when he came in late that night. With one last look around, she left.

At the bank she drew out money from a trust fund left to her by her parents, and then the taxi took her to Miami International Airport.

By the time the jet was thundering down the runway she had convinced herself that with miles separating her and Alex their relationship would die a quick and relatively painless death. Once she reached California and found a place to live she intended to continue her education and eventually file for divorce. Yes, this was definitely the best way, she thought as she watched the ground falling away from the window of the aircraft. She was sure when Alex got the necessary papers he would be relieved to be off the hook. If they ever ran into each other again, well, he might even thank her. If not with some outright spoken words, then maybe with just a look that said it.

The plane climbed steadily higher. Sara closed her eyes, remembering she hadn't slept much the night before. In a few moments her head lolled to the side and she slept during the entire flight to California, exhausted from the emotional turmoil plaguing her.

Chapter 1

The group of men in the office of the Narcotics Division of the Miami Police Department gathered into a tight, intimate knot. The four of them, all in their mid-thirties, were dressed in business suits. Used to working and socializing together, they enjoyed an easy camaraderie most of the time, but one of the men stood out in the group. With a lazy, smooth, rhythmic manner of speaking, Alex Cordera dominated the group with ease and good reason. He was the boss. In just seven years he had worked his way up from homicide detective to the head of an elite unit in the Narcotics Division. But right now, there was a glazed, weary look in his eyes.

It had been a lousy week. They had been sorting through tedious details for almost an hour. Alex had been ticking off things in his mind before he let his men go for the weekend.

"So you checked out that latest lead on Raphael Cruzero down in the Grove?"

"A dead end. The guy didn't know what he was talking about. He was just hustling for a handout."

"Nothing we can use from the wiretap on his phone?"

"Nothing. From his telephone conversations he is only what he appears to be—a highly successful businessman."

"But we know he's behind some of the largest shipments coming into Miami. So far, he hasn't put a foot wrong, but when he does, we're going to nail him." Alex jabbed his finger to emphasize his point, thinking to himself that getting Raphael Cruzero was becoming almost an obsession with him. They had so little on Cruzero. But Alex considered himself and his men to be the best at what they did, and they'd get him. He didn't like it when some flashy-looking criminal thought he could outthink him, outmaneuver him. He relaxed against the edge of his desk for a moment, then turned to Mike Garcia.

"What's happening to our informants? Is somebody paying them more than we are?" His hard-edged humor came to his rescue.

"Nothing's happened to them," Rocky Lucas answered for Mike, shrugging. "Nobody knows anything. It's quiet on the street about Cruzero. He moves in more elevated circles. Nobody knows nothing. He's also Colombian," Rocky reminded.

"I know." Alex expelled a ragged sigh of agreement. "He only deals with Colombians and we haven't got enough Colombian undercover agents to go around. It's the old story."

Alex reached into his pocket for a cigarette, drew one out and lit it. He kept himself down to one pack a week, which wasn't too bad, he reflected, then turned his thoughts to the unit he directed. Its name, Centac, was an abbreviation for central tactical unit. They worked with various government agencies and had an impressive record for putting away high-level drug traffickers. Alex enjoyed the privilege of being able to pick and choose cases, to target certain individuals, unlike detectives in other divisions. Raphael Cruzero had come to their attention because of his success and background and because of some of the people he associated with. They had been investigating him for more than a year, though the investigation was only one of several Centac worked on during that period. He was a puzzling figure. So far Centac had uncovered blind trusts in the Bahamas and a shell corporation in Panama, places where they thought he laundered money gained from large cocaine shipments. They couldn't find out anything else about his operation that would stand up in court. Colombian drug dealers were always hard setups to infiltrate, because Colombians worked only for Colombians. And because reprisals were swift and harsh, it was hard to get them to talk.

"It's been one of those weeks it's better to forget about. Come on, it's time we were all out of here," Alex concluded, stabbing out the half-smoked cigarette.

"We should have been out of here two hours ago," Rocky Lucas pointed out dryly.

Alex smiled to himself, knowing Lucas had just made a valid observation. As usual, they'd been working late. "All right, we work long hours, but we get results. We're the best." Alex shrugged into his jacket and adjusted his tie, waiting for any challenge to that comment. There was none; they all knew what he said was the truth. He smiled to himself and picked up his keys from his desk. Gary Torres took his hands out of his pockets and pushed away from the door-jamb. Mike Garcia unwound his stocky frame from the chair he was sprawled in.

"My wife is really looking forward to your sister's wedding tomorrow, Alex. She blew the balance in the checking account to get a new dress. This is going to be some wedding," he announced.

Reminded of his sister's wedding, Alex checked his wristwatch. "I was supposed to pick up my tuxedo today. I don't want to have to pick it up tomorrow morning because I'm going out tonight."

Mike Garcia couldn't suppress a broad, knowing grin, and neither could the other detectives in the unit. Alex's men knew him well. When he said he was going out for the night, he meant it literally. He never got in until the next morning and often stopped to eat breakfast on the way home.

"Where're you getting it from?"

"Quintero's in Little Havana."

"Quintero stays open late. If you leave right now you can still catch him."

The four of them started walking at a brisk pace through the Narcotics Division toward the bank of elevators. Alex had worked with these men for several years; they were almost like family. Like him, Mike Garcia and Gary Torres were Cuban, but there was a subtle difference between himself and the other two,

Alex thought pensively. They were second generation, not born on Cuban soil as he had been. A little bit of Cuba still remained in his blood and Alex always silently acknowledged it. Bilingual and Americanized, he was equally at home in Miami's established Anglo circles and in Little Havana. Someone had once described him as a kind of unassimilated yuppie with a foot planted firmly in each community, he remembered, amused.

Mike Garcia turned to him in the elevator, joking. "Alex, you better not roll out of Marita's bed too late in the morning. If you're late for your own sister's wedding, Lourdis will never let you forget it."

Alex smiled to himself with unrepentant macho charm. He never let what a woman thought inhibit his conduct too much; a man could get into a lot of trouble if he did.

He turned his head toward Mike. "What do you think of my sister marrying the former prosecutor extraordinaire?" His prospective brother-in-law had made the big switch and gone over to the "other side." Now, instead of prosecuting drug traffickers, he was defending them in court for fat fees. "Maybe I *should* be late for my sister's wedding when she's marrying a rogue like that. Sometimes I think there's no real justice in this world." He tossed the keys to his Jaguar into the air and caught them.

"No, you got it all wrong, man," Mike flashed back. "There's plenty of justice out there. The more money you got the more justice you get."

"Let's go." Alex grinned at his sharp-witted friend. It wasn't the first time he had heard that kind of remark and it wouldn't be the last. In his present weary frame of wind he could almost believe it, but he knew he felt jaded, and at such times the war on drugs could seem like nothing but a big game. "After a week like this one, we deserve some R and R. We've earned ourselves a big break."

Outside in the parking lot he slid into his hunter-green Jaguar. A flick of the wrist and the car's engine sprang to life. In moments the car surged out of the parking lot to join the mainstream traffic, which was always heavy in Miami no matter what the time of day. He was glad it was Friday. All week long he had worked with the frustrating sensation that he was getting nowhere fast. Still, he knew from experience that that was often when something really big or unusual turned up.

He eased the car to a stop at the traffic light and let his gaze follow a bunch of pedestrians crossing the street. Milestones like a wedding in the family made a man stop and think, take stock of himself whether he wanted to or not. After tomorrow he would be the only one in the family who wasn't married. Well, he had been married once, if you could call that six-week fiasco with Sara Langston a marriage. Few people outside his immediate family knew that he had ever been married at all. He liked it that way. A man didn't want all of Miami to know he had made a fool of himself over a woman. That was the way he remembered his brief marital encounter with Sara Langston. He had tried to do the right thing. For that he had gotten screwed. Their marriage had lasted a mind-bending six weeks, and he had known her for maybe six weeks before that. Three months, tops, they had

been together—not what you would call an enduring
relationship. Sara was a real piece of work, all right.

The light changed and he shifted smoothly into gear.
For the hundredth time he reminded himself that when
he discovered she was only nineteen he should have
walked away. But there was something about her that
had drawn him, held him, and he had never been able
to walk away or keep his hands off her. Had anyone
ever been able to explain satisfactorily why a man
wanted one woman more than another?

Leftover feelings, never vented, continued to well up
inside him. The cooler American side of his nature
told him it was all water under the bridge; he had forgotten about it long ago. But the fiery Cuban side said
if he ever ran into her again there was a little score to
settle. She had wounded him deeply. His fierce male
pride had never been vindicated and no self-respecting
Cuban let any woman get away with that.

The huge atrium soared hundreds of feet overhead
in the grand hotel. Scattered around its blue slate
floors were large, round linen-swathed tables where
wedding guests sat enjoying what was left of a lavish
banquet. After dessert, coffee and liqueurs there
would be dancing in a nearby reception room with an
open bar and two alternating bands, salsa and rock.

Leaning against the wall with his hands in his tuxedo pants pockets, Alex watched a glassed-in elevator
crawling slowly up the atrium's marble wall. Bore-
dom swamped his senses. He got bored too quickly
and too easily these days, he realized. For a moment
he wondered if his sister, Lourdis, hadn't been right
when she told him on one occasion his job was bru-

talizing him. He was always looking for excitement. Was he getting hooked on the adrenaline highs and lows, the excitement inherent in his work? Was he developing a jaundiced outlook toward people and life because of the kind of work he did? Sometimes he thought the only time he was really happy was when he had just arrested some drug trafficker. Was nailing individuals like Raphael Cruzero becoming an obsession, or were he and his men only coping with the pressures of a demanding and often unrewarding, difficult job the only way they knew how? He thought of the two men in his unit already divorced. He didn't have any simple answers to his questions, so he shunted them off to one side of his mind. A white-jacketed waiter passed with a tray of drinks, and Alex signaled to him. The waiter altered his course and paused in front of him, offering a glass of champagne.

Over the rim of the glass he saw his sister, the social climber of the family. She was a vision of loveliness in an heirloom-lace mantilla and yards and yards of silk organza. With the train of her gown draped over her arm, she walked toward him. "Well, what do you think?" Her dark luminous eyes indicated the lavish reception.

A corner of his mouth lifted as he teased his sister with smooth sardonic wit. "Very elegant, very expensive. Big bucks have changed hands. Is the groom paying for all this?"

"Leo offered to split the bill with us."

"Where is he?"

She looked over her shoulder. "Over there somewhere, talking to one of his associates." Alex's eyes followed hers. For his sister's sake, he kept his feelings regarding her husband to himself.

Turning her attention back to her brother, Lourdis smiled warmly. "You'll never guess who I ran into the other day."

"Well, if I'm never going to guess, you might as well tell me." His amused expression told her he was still engaging in a little brotherly teasing.

"I ran into Sara's sister. We used to attend the same college," she reminded him. Then she added casually, "Did you know that Sara has been working overseas for the past five years as a photographer with *World Photographic?*"

For a moment he smiled at some distant point in space at the irony in her words. Then his gaze swung back to her face, to answer her question with one of his own. "Do you think someone who walked out on me without a word, someone who left me a four-line note, is going to fill me in on what she has been doing with her life for the past five years? Lourdis, I always thought you were smarter than that." She *was* smarter than that, and they both knew it.

"Linda said she's tired of traveling, that she's coming home for good."

The words *coming home for good* made something inside Alex quicken and smolder. The smile on his face disguised it, but his eyes burned with the news of Sara's return. "What do you want me to do?" he said. "Maybe you think I should go and welcome her back."

"I thought you might be interested. That's all." His sister shrugged her slender bare shoulders innocently.

"Listen good." He jabbed his finger at her. "When she walked out on me, that was the end."

"Is Sara the reason why you never remarried?" she asked slyly.

"You want to know the real reason why I never got married again?" He smiled. "Just between you and me, Lourdis, it's because I like getting laid."

His sister's eyes widened at her brother's plunge into vulgarity. "That's street talk. That job, the kind of people you mix with, they're changing you, making you callous and cynical. Everyone in the family thinks so. You never used to talk like that."

Alex quirked an eyebrow at her. "It offends you? The way I talk offends you? Then from now on keep that beautiful nose out of my business and you won't hear any more talk that offends you." The jabbing finger tapped her nose affectionately, but the hard-edged look in his eyes reminded her he meant business.

Leaving his sister standing there bemused and suffering from an attack of feminine pique, Alex turned and walked toward the bar. There was a satisfied smile on his face, laughter darkening his eyes, at the expression on his sister's face. You had to assert yourself with women like Lourdis or they walked all over you. You had to draw lines and show them how far they could go or they started interfering in the way you ran your life. But his sister's words regarding Sara came back to him. *Forget it,* he warned himself. It's over.

Only a few weeks after she returned from working overseas, Sara went out to dinner with a group of her

friends to a restaurant in Coconut Grove—and a page
out of the past bounced back into her life. When her
father worked for Banco America, he had moved his
family around the South American continent. One of
the countries they had lived in for many years was
Colombia. While in Colombia they had become fast
friends with a family named Cruzero. She and Raphael Cruzero had spent their early adolescence next
door to each other. But when they literally bumped
into each other in the crowded restaurant on the way
to their respective tables, she and Raphael didn't recognize each other immediately. Both politely excused
themselves and started to move away, then they froze
in their tracks and did an about-face.

The taller-than-average, solidly built man with thick
dark wavy hair and a very strong-featured face surveyed her more closely. For a moment Sara stared
back at him. Then the stranger's face split into a wide
two-thousand-watt Colombian smile. "Sara?"

In an explosion of surprise she cried his name.
"Raphael!"

They hastily excused themselves from their parties
and spent the rest of the evening catching up on the
intervening years.

When Sara walked into the exclusive Polo Lounge
and restaurant with Raphael a few weeks later to celebrate his birthday, they had dated several times and
were already on more than friendly terms. She had
been looking forward to the evening all week. Wearing a black lace outfit with a sweetheart neckline that
plunged to expose the deep cleft of her breasts, she
knew she was looking her best. Her high-heeled pumps
enabled her to look directly into Raphael's eyes.

"I have asked the waiter to seat us here so that we can sit next to each other." His whispered words fanned the side of her face. Waiters hovered around them as they sank into a plush banquette. She watched him ease himself down beside her. He played tennis three times a week and was very fit. Leaning forward, he clasped her hand in his raised fist, smiling at her over his knuckles. A waiter produced champagne, and their conversation continued as he eased the cork out of a champagne bottle with a deft touch.

"Sara, have you ever been back to Colombia?"

"I stopped in Panama and Argentina, but I never got back to Colombia."

"Do you remember much about it? Would you like to see how much it has changed?"

"I'd love to see it all again. I hear where we used to live has changed a lot."

"That is true." He was suddenly serious. "Come back with me, Sara. Let me show Colombia to you all over again."

She looked into his eyes, perpetually mischievous gleaming dark pools, and considered his invitation. But she didn't answer. His thick dark wavy hair shone under the recessed lighting. The wide smile spreading across the strong Colombian features told her he was after something.

"It's only a few hours by plane. I travel back and forth all the time on business. I could rent a plane and we could go for a long weekend. We could fly there at our convenience, travel wherever you want to go— Bogatá, Cali, Cartagena."

"If you weren't such a good friend and I didn't know you so well I might say this sounds like a prop-

osition.'' She knew if she traveled with him alone he
would expect her to sleep with him.

"But I insist that we invite your charming and very
beautiful sister, too.'' His eyes danced with silent
laughter.

"Well, since you insist—'' she laughed deep in her
throat ''—I promise to ask her.''

"Make sure you don't forget,'' he countered. There
was a look of would-be possession in Raphael's eyes
that she didn't know if she wanted to encourage. Ap-
parently satisfied for the moment, he decided it was
time to sample the excellent champagne.

"A toast to my birthday,'' he announced, urging her
to pick up the crystal flute in front of her. Their glasses
clinked delicately.

The toast reminded Sara of something she wanted
to ask him. "What would you like for your birthday?
You still haven't told me. You said you would.''

As he put down the glass of champagne, his dark
eyes bored deep into hers with a mixture of deep affection and some pure unadulterated lust. "I would
like it very much if you'd kiss me right now, here in the
middle of the Polo Lounge.''

"Mmm,'' she murmured, pretending to mull it over
in her mind. "I suppose that is a reasonable request,
seeing it's your birthday. Are you sure you don't want
anything else?'' Her eyes widened innocently.

He shrugged. "That is a very leading question. But
for the time being . . . I am content.''

Silver bangles encasing her forearm clinked together musically as her hand closed around his striped
silk tie. His laughing eyes challenged her, goading her
on. Boldly pulling him toward her, she grazed her lips

across his. It hardly qualified as a kiss, but Raphael might have mistaken it for a sensual tease, a promise of something to come, a more genuine kiss in a more private place. But ever since she had known Raphael, he had been quick to capitalize on any situation and so it was now. He seized the back of her head, and holding her lips locked beneath his, he took firm possession of her mouth. Instantly the kiss hardened with a searing pressure, parting her lips until it became a full-blown kiss of passion. The hot hunger of it lengthened. When he finally released her they drew slowly apart. For a moment he gazed into her eyes and she into his. The silent message he relayed was unmistakable; he wanted total possession. The slowly dawning realization that they might have attracted some unwanted attention made Sara turn to check out the room around her. Two men were approaching the table. Their approach was like an action replay in a televised sports event; the movements of the players slowed down by the camera speed so that the viewers could observe each detail more closely.

Shock was slowing everything down for Sara. Everything faded around her but the sight of two men approaching their table. Sounds dimmed and colors blurred. At first she thought she was seeing things. But when she realized she wasn't, her heart began to pound with soft, heavy, alarming thuds. She felt the impulse to get up and leave but found she couldn't move at all and remained frozen in her seat. She couldn't even tear her gaze away. She didn't recognize one of the men, but the other was her ex-husband, Alex Cordera.

Raphael's sensitive antennae picked up immediately on the dramatic change in her demeanor. His gaze flicked to her face, then bounded away from the silent woman next to him to address the two men who had reached the table and stood hovering over them.

"Lieutenant Cordera, Detective Garcia. Are you here on business or can you join us for a drink?"

A painfully familiar, accented voice crossed the small space separating Sara from her ex-husband. "We're working tonight—we can only stay a few minutes. The waiter told us it was your birthday, so we came over to offer our congratulations. *Feliz cumpleaños.*"

Sara sat in stunned silence. Darkly handsome, broad-shouldered and powerfully built, Alex was still a magnet. Seven years had done nothing to diminish the impact he had on her. She felt exposed, strangely vulnerable, as if she had suddenly found herself without any clothes on in a room full of people. Alex looked at her, his burnt sienna eyes burning holes in her face.

"This is my very good friend, Sara Langston," Raphael said to the men, then addressed Sara. "Sometimes Lieutenant Cordera and Detective Garcia come to me to check out a lead on someone who has paid cash for an expensive car from one of my showrooms. They work for the Narcotics Division at the Miami Police Department," he explained to her.

Alex was quick to correct the mistaken impression. "Sara and I have already met. Haven't we, Sara?"

With her heart still pounding she regained her powers of speech. "That's right. We have."

"More than once. Isn't that right?" He prodded with the mesmerizing stare.

Unconsciously holding her breath, she injected a forced lightness into her tone. "Yes."

"You two know each other well, Sara?" Raphael asked, obviously surprised.

She sent Alex a look that begged him to play along. Their brief marriage wasn't something she wanted dragged out now; she would tell Raphael about it some other time, some other place.

"It was a long time ago. But we were good friends for a while," she said.

She watched Alex close his eyes briefly. A broad smile crept across his face as if she had said something very funny and he was savoring the humor of it.

"Sara, is that the way you would describe our former relationship—*we were good friends for a while?* Can't you come up with a better description than that of our former *relationship?*"

His eyes locked onto hers with smiling menace, an expression that told her he was out for blood. What was the matter with him? Why was he acting this way? She tried to figure it out but there was no time. The only thing she could do now was play down whatever he said, minimize it.

"I suppose we were more than friends . . . but I was only nineteen. It didn't last very long and we certainly didn't see very much of each other." Her eyes flashed a warning look that said "back off," but Alex had never been receptive to a woman telling him anything and he continued to ignore her.

"You're right about that. It didn't last long. But you're mistaken when you say we didn't see much of each other. I remember seeing a lot of you and I remember it all very well."

Alex let a wandering, very male look drop pointedly to the shadowy cleft of her breasts, the smiling
menace continuing as it traveled slowly back to her
face. The heavy innuendo behind his words conjured
up vivid pictures in her mind of both of them in bed
naked, the raw turbulence of his passion, his body
covering, then pumping rhythmically into hers. She
watched his eyes glow with hard-won satisfaction as
she began to color. The heat flush crept slowly over her
skin beneath the black lace, crawling up her neck until it reached her cheekbones.

"Sara and I are old 'friends,' too. Isn't that true,
Sara?"

She turned to look at Raphael blankly for a fleeting moment, still reeling, until his question finally
clicked in her mind.

"Oh, yes. Our families knew each other in Colombia. Raphael and I spent many happy times together.
We've been seeing each other ever since I got back."

The word *friend* was taking on varying shades of
meaning, but the bottom line seemed to be ultimate
sexual possession. When she saw the look exchanged
between the two men, Sara suddenly felt as though she
were some kind of bone being fought over as disturbing undercurrents flew back across the table.

Compelling as always, Alex commandeered her attention again easily. "Why are you back in Miami?"

"I haven't broken the law by coming back, have I?
Why do you want to know?" Her accusing stare focused on his face.

"If you are here to stay for good I want to welcome
you back, Sara, no other reason." The lazy amiable
smile spread across his face, making him look about

as innocent as a cat with a canary locked in its jaws, while his words suggested she should have thought twice about coming back onto his turf.

"I'm sure we would all have a great time getting to know one another better, but Detective Garcia and I have to go. It was nice meeting you again, Sara. Enjoy your birthday, Raphael." After exchanging farewells the detectives left the side of the table. Sara didn't watch Alex go; instead she took a fortifying sip of champagne.

With a gleam in his eyes Raphael turned back to her. "What was between you two?"

Sara heard herself murmuring some dismissive remarks. She knew her reply didn't satisfy the shrewd man sitting next to her. But unlike her ex-husband, Raphael had no desire to watch her squirm and didn't pursue the subject any further.

Outside the Polo Lounge Mike Garcia let out a long hissing sound through his teeth, then exploded into laughter. "That is one good-looking woman. Did you see the look on Cruzero's face when you said you knew her? I wouldn't mind being in Raphael Cruzero's shoes tonight."

The remark dug at Alex but he didn't like to admit it.

"What was between you two anyway?"

"Not much. We were married once. That's all."

Mike Garcia whistled softly. "Uh-oh. No one could have figured on this. What are you going to do now?"

"If I have any sense I'm going to stay away from her and keep my hands in my pockets. Something I should have done seven years ago," Alex retorted in a low voice.

"You still dig her?"

"What do you think?" Alex laughed softly at his own reaction.

"I think you got competition. Just how good friends would you say she and Cruzero are?"

"With Sara you never know," Alex fired back, then shot Mike a look that said loud and clear he didn't want to talk about his ex-wife anymore. "Come on. Let's get out of here." The two men climbed into the parked car, slamming the doors simultaneously.

Mike drove and Alex sank into the passenger seat. But Mike's question along with a lot of other thoughts were gnawing at Alex's mind like a dog worrying a bone. The sight of Sara sitting next to Raphael Cruzero had hit him like a hard blow to the stomach. The sight of Cruzero kissing her had been like emotional dynamite going off inside him. From the moment his eyes locked onto her face the passionate Cuban side of his nature had taken control, reacting sharply, almost violently. A mixture of feelings had driven him over to their table when he knew he should have stayed away.

Just how good *friends* were they? His eyes narrowed on the passing traffic. The way Raphael's eyes had issued a subtle warning left no doubt in his mind about what Cruzero wanted. It was a warning to stay away; Cruzero thought of her as his own private reserve. How far had the relationship advanced? That was anybody's guess. Sara had sat there, looking more striking, more tempting now than she had ever been. It was a blow to his male ego that he could still find a woman who had walked out on him so attractive. For that reason alone he had enjoyed watching her squirm. Alex sank deeper into the car seat, brooding, considering all the angles.

His thoughts shifted to Raphael. Of all the men in Miami, why did she have to get mixed up with Raphael Cruzero? He reviewed the conversation; she had known him from Colombia. He remembered Sara telling him when they were together how her father had worked around the South American continent, moving his family from place to place. He agreed with Mike—no one could have figured on this, he thought wearily. He reached into his pocket for a cigarette, then clicked open his metal lighter. Cruzero was a man he had vowed to get, a target his men were homing in on. Tonight he was faced with an even more compelling reason for tracking him down. Disturbing, conflicting feelings eddied back and forth inside him that he didn't want to identify or examine too closely. Seeing his ex-wife in Raphael Cruzero's presence had intensified them, overheated them.

His mind skipped to her reaction to him. Something had flared in her eyes when she first saw him. He paused to light the cigarette, inhaling deeply as he let the lighter clink shut slowly. There had been startled recognition in her eyes, but that was only natural; he had expected that. He had taken her completely by surprise. But there was something else he hadn't expected. Charged depths. There were charged depths in her eyes, coupled with apprehension, a look of vulnerability. Was it only because of the past? The answer came to him without any struggle. It was because the magic was still there between them, undeniably, blatantly there. That was why. She had sensed it as immediately as he had. There was no point in kidding himself about that.

Alex sprawled his powerful frame deeper into the seat, smiling to himself. Then abruptly, he sat up and turned to Mike. "Drop me off at the next corner. I feel like walking the rest of the way."

The car slowed down, cruising next to the curb. Mike watched silently as Alex opened the door, got out and slammed the door shut. For a moment Alex stood watching the red taillights of the car recede down the street, then studied the glow of the burning cigarette tip between his fingers.

That apprehension he saw in Sara's eyes goaded him on, touching something deep inside him. It was a reaction that sharpened all his predatory male instincts. Instinctive drives were strong in him, he was well aware of that. There was the killer instinct that made him go after men like Raphael Cruzero with undivided ruthlessness. Then there was the other instinct, equally strong if not stronger, which said a real man never let a woman diminish his manhood in any way. A sense of long overdue vindication was on his mind and aimed at his ex-wife.

Chapter 2

Sara joined her sister, who she had moved in with, and two of their friends at the Country and Western Tavern on Friday night after work. When they stepped inside the bar, complete with sawdust on the floors, the twang of electric guitars hung in the air, competing with the dull roar of voices and laughter. On a small spotlighted stage, two young women dressed in white fringed jackets sang a duet with their faces close together, accompanying themselves on guitars. Their combined voices twanged loudly into the microphone, which had a faint echo to it, lamenting a world filled with two-timin' men with cheatin' hearts.

Jammed with people from all walks of life, many of them dressed in western-style clothing, the honky-tonk quickly lived up to its reputation of being as wild as the wild West, Sara thought, smiling to herself. There were some rough-looking guys and some mean-looking women, but there was also a strong yuppie element escaping from the button-down-collar straight life. People stood three and four deep at the bar waiting to be served.

In a few moments Sara and her companions were engaged in conversation with two men who looked as though they had stepped straight out of the Marlboro ad. One was an accountant from Fort Lauderdale, the other a building contractor from Miami. The conversation was lively, and easygoing banter flowed back and forth. Lulled by the music and the congenial company, Sara didn't mind being bumped into constantly in the crowded bar. So she paid little attention when she sensed a man's presence close behind her, until suddenly a pair of hands clamped onto her hips. The presence closed in on her—he was pressing intimately against her back, his breath fanning her neck. Something about those hands made warning bells go off inside her mind. There was magic in those hands, bringing back another time, another place. Her heartbeat accelerated dramatically and she had to force herself to slowly turn around. Alex stood over her, taunting her with a lazy smile.

"Remember me, Sara? Your ex-husband?"

Feeling like someone who had momentarily lost contact with reality, she could only gaze silently into his eyes.

"You and I need to talk, Sara."

"About what?"

"We have plenty to talk about," he whispered in her ear. "This time we're going to say it face-to-face, not through our respective lawyers." She felt his hand at the lower part of her back, prompting her to walk ahead of him.

"Why couldn't you have put on twenty or thirty pounds? Why do you have to be like you are?" he whispered, taking in her black suede skirt and high-heeled cowboy boots.

"You haven't changed either," she retorted. "You're still the same arrogant bastard you always were." His hand prodded, propelling her along by a formidable combination of male strength and smoldering macho heat.

"You owe me an apology for the way you behaved at the Polo Lounge."

"*I* owe *you* an apology? You have that all wrong, Sara." He laughed softly. Allowing her no time to recover, he navigated them through the smoke-filled atmosphere, through the crush of people toward a dimly visible set of fire doors. The Exit sign glowed red in the dark over her head.

"Where are we going?" she demanded.

He replied by pushing her not-too-gently through the exit. Once outside, she turned to confront him. Whatever he wanted, she resented the way she had been manhandled out the door, wrenched away from her companions.

"Aren't your friends going to wonder where you went?" Uncharacteristic sarcasm edged her words.

The fire doors clanged shut behind them. Alex stood over her, looking much as she remembered him from the Polo Lounge—magnetic, darkly handsome and doing one of his famous slow burns with a look in his eyes that said he had a score to settle.

"It's quieter out here and more private."

"What do you want?" she murmured warily.

"I told you we have to talk about a few things," he replied. With his hands locked on her shoulders he backed her against the cool brick wall. The breadth of his shoulders blotted out the view of the parking lot behind him.

"You remember now that I'm your ex-husband. I'm glad to see that when we're alone your memory improves." She watched his eyes grow lazy, three-quarter-lidded with the humor of his own words. "It's nice that you do me the courtesy of remembering that we were once married, Sara."

He was making a reference to that night at the Polo Lounge when she had pretended otherwise. "I was on a date. I didn't want to be embarrassed by the past," she explained patiently.

Alex's deceptive humor and calm instantly vanished. Pure vitriol flashed into his eyes. "Our marriage was an embarrassment? Was I an embarrassment, Sara? Is that what you're saying?" he shouted at her.

But Sara was no longer nineteen and not easily intimidated. "You're twisting my words," she accused.

Suddenly, he pulled the black Stetson she was wearing off her head. Honey-blond hair tumbled around her face. The suddenness of the action jarred her nerves because of the deep anger motivating it. But she was bewildered as to why. She watched him toss the hat aside.

"What did you do that for?"

"I want to take a good look at the woman who walked out on me seven years ago. You know something, Sara, I should have embarrassed you in front of your 'friend.'"

"You did embarrass me. I didn't enjoy being looked over like some streetwalker. You were lewd and insulting."

"I have every reason to embarrass you. You walked out on me." He jabbed a finger at her nose. "That was embarrassing for me, that was embarrassing for my family. Did you ever think how I felt? Do you think I enjoyed being informed through the United States mail that you had no more use for me? Adios and four lousy lines. I deserved more than that, Sara. Maybe you think I had no feelings. Maybe you think I got bounced around on the football field one too many times. Maybe you think because I'm Hispanic I'm thick between the ears."

"That's not what I think," she flared back, her own voice rising. His hands bit into the soft flesh of her upper arms, jerking her forward sharply so that their eyes and lips were only inches apart. The dizzying fear that he was going to lose control completely flashed through her.

"You want to know what I thought? I thought you would be relieved. I thought you would be glad to be off the hook. That's what I thought!" she cried softly.

The intensity of his eyes only deepened with blazing humor. He seemed to find that funny. He stared at her in a kind of angry rapture. "So you thought you could read my mind, Sara? If you're so good at reading my mind maybe you can tell me something. Why did you think I married you? Because I didn't have anything better to do that day?" he concluded in a low roar.

"That's not what I thought."

"In case you didn't understand, let me explain it to you. I was trying to do the right thing and, and you left me feeling like some dumb jerk with his cajones cut off."

She had had enough. In a voice that vibrated with feline fury she attacked. "Maybe I didn't want you to do the *right thing*. Did you ever think that? Maybe I didn't want you to do me any *big favors!*"

She tried to wrench free of his grip. But he hung on with grim ferocity. A muscle leaped in his jaw as the fake smile returned with a vengeance. "Tell me something. Did you decide that you didn't want me to do the right thing *before* or *after* the miscarriage?"

"After—"

"When you didn't need me anymore!"

He wasn't listening to anything she said. Looking into his face Sara felt as if she had stumbled into a highly charged magnetic field; the power of his anger surged at her in waves now. Confused by it, buffeted by it, bewildered by it, she stared transfixed. But suddenly she realized what he was really angry about. She folded her arms in front of her.

"So that's what all this is about—your colossal macho pride was stung. Maybe you should have kept your hands off me. Then you wouldn't have felt compelled to do the 'right thing' and your colossal macho pride would still be intact! I'm glad I didn't stick around and dwindle into some pale shadow of a wife paying you back for doing the 'right thing' for the rest of my life."

"So you didn't want to dwindle into my pale shadow of a wife. You're reading my mind again, and you still got it all wrong, Sara. I wanted a woman. But that is something you wouldn't know anything about. You know why?''

"I have this strange feeling you're going to tell me."

"You don't know how to be a woman. That's why," he shouted at her, his words cutting to the quick.

"Maybe you should have given me a chance to become one," she flared back with sweet sarcasm.

"You are right about that. I should have kept my hands off you when I found out you were only nineteen." He held up his hands in a hands-off gesture, and she watched a vindictive look crawl into his eyes. "But you're older now and I've got nothing lined up for tonight." He lifted his chin, letting his gaze slide down to her breasts. "What do you say? You want to make it with me tonight?"

Her hand lashed out instantly, a reflex action, connecting with his jaw. Alex retaliated with split-second timing, locking her in his rough embrace. Imprisoning her in his arms with brutal strength, he studied her face. His eyes burned her with a fiery absorption. Sara twisted her head sideways but he forced her face slowly, inexorably back to him with his free hand, his fingers digging into the smooth skin of her face.

When he had her in position he clamped his mouth on hers in a driving, bruising kiss, forcing her lips apart with no preliminaries. He kissed her as a man would kiss a whore, using his tongue like a rapier. It was clear to her what he wanted to do. He was bent on humiliating her the way he felt she had humiliated him. He took what he wanted and dealt out more of the same. Nothing she did had any effect. Her arms imprisoned, she lashed out several punishing blows to his shins with the heel of a cowboy boot.

Quickly putting an end to her rebellion, he pinned her against the wall with his body, his powerful frame engulfing hers, imprisoning her legs with his far more powerful ones. As cars came off the highway, the jeweled eeriness of their headlight beams swept over them. Burying his face in the silky sweetness of her hair and the curve of her neck, he slid his hand underneath the suede miniskirt. Grasping a handful of flesh inside lacy bikinis he thrust her into the hardening bulge between his legs.

"You pass the test for being female, honey," he breathed harshly into her ear. "There's undeniable proof. But I still have my doubts about you ever making it as a woman."

Raw desire crawled through her legs and arms, then plunged deep into her groin in a downward draining spiral, ending in a primitive tug of arousal that turned her thighs to jelly. Dismayed by her reaction to this rough treatment, but overwhelmed momentarily, she closed her eyes, gasping softly at the searing sensation. Then she turned her head in to the corded muscles of his neck so that he couldn't see her face. But the steel grip of his fingers twisted her face back underneath his perusal. There was no escape. She saw the dark satisfaction filter into his eyes. Humiliation stung her cheeks, but she knew her gray eyes glittered with arousal. A heavy thickening silence stretched between them.

"Are you satisfied now?" she breathed shakily. "Have you salvaged some of your twisted pride?"

"Maybe," he whispered cryptically, pressing his palms against the brick wall on either side of her face. He peered down at her in the dark with his mouth only inches from hers in a characteristic stance of domination. "Sara, there was a time when whatever you asked for, I would have gone out and tried to get it for you. Now, I would think twice about giving you the time of day."

If he had intended to wound her, to humiliate her, he had more than succeeded. For a long moment she couldn't say anything at all. Tears stung the backs of her eyes. But it was more than her life was worth to let him see them, or even worse, to give in to them. She turned abruptly away on the pretext of finding her hat. Walking over toward it, she stooped to retrieve it.

"Tell me something. Did you enjoy roughing me up?" she accused bitterly.

"Roughing you up? You call that roughing you up?" He laughed softly, jeering at her remark. "You ought to come into my world and see what roughing up means."

She slipped the Stetson back on her head, adjusting the chin strap. Then, mustering her tattered pride, she addressed him with an accusing look in her eyes. "Your world has turned you into a revoltingly crude man. Maybe you ought to think about changing your job."

"There was a time when you didn't think I was revolting or crude. Or have you forgotten that?" His eyes drilled lazily for an answer.

"That was a long time ago. Now, I can't wait to wash the feel of your hands off me."

"So, you think you can't wait to get the feel of my hands off you." Lazy soft laughter echoed on the heels of his words, belying the hardening aspect of his eyes. "You're lying to yourself and to me, Sara," he announced softly. "There's still plenty going on between you and me, whether either one of us wants to admit it, and with or without Raphael sniffing around."

The truth stung. Sara struggled to get a grip on the composure that eluded her. When his hands were on her the naked truth had been undeniable. This impassioned man standing over her with the knowing eyes could still arouse her just as much as she could still arouse him. She couldn't explain why, but she knew he was right. She watched Alex's eyes glaze over with the sharp irony of their situation.

He pounded on the fire doors until someone yanked them open from inside. "We better get back inside. It's dangerous for you out here." His tone underscored the meaning that he still wasn't entirely in control of his feelings.

With her head held high from stung pride, she walked in front of him, weaving her way back through the smoky, noisy club until she rejoined the group of people she had arrived with. She felt as though she was shaking in her boots. Alex had always had that effect on her.

Darting a glance over her shoulder to confirm that he was going to leave her alone, she watched him walk away. In a few moments he had joined his friends on the other side of the bar. Studiously ignoring his presence, she joined in the conversation, ignoring her sister's questioning look. But inside she was still quaking from a mixture of feelings she couldn't easily explain away. The one person in the world who could really rattle her had walked back into her life. With devastating ease Alex had fanned back to life feelings that she had thought were long buried.

Assiduously ignoring her, Alex was talking to a dark-haired young woman who hung on his every word. The men in his entourage were making out like bandits, all detectives, hardworking, hard playing. With wounded pride she turned back to her group, convinced it was now over. He had spent his anger, salvaged his colossal pride by humiliating her, traded insult for insult, accusation for accusation. What more could he want? Now that they had gotten the seemingly inevitable out of the way, maybe they could both get on with their lives.

But a strange sensual buzz of excitement remained, along with the imprint of his bruising kisses. The relentless pressure of his mouth, the feel of his hands urging her into the hard vitality of his male body had been burned into her mind.

The sizzling effect of Alex's presence left her feeling as if she were on fire or had a bad case of sunburn and she was disoriented by it for the rest of the evening. His remark that there was still a lot going on between them continued to reverberate through her.

Alex stood outside the Country and Western Tavern, lighting a cigarette and mulling things over in his mind. He was still burning with unrequited passion toward his ex-wife. Physically aroused, emotionally aroused, he didn't thank her for this explosion of emotions with no satisfaction in sight. A plan was

forming in his mind, fueled by the passion he was re-
luctantly discovering he still felt for her.

He already knew Cruzero wanted her, and Alex
wanted Cruzero and Sara. *Why not go after both at
the same time?* he thought as he studied the burning
embers of his cigarette. He knew he was still spoiling
for revenge; the anger wasn't out of him. The humiliation he had just dealt out to his ex had only stirred up
emotions he hadn't known were there.

He still wanted her. Damned if he didn't still want
her, he thought, throwing the glowing butt away. It
was a blow to his pride to admit it. When she was in
his arms he was like a man possessed. He wasn't in
control of his emotions. That was dangerous. If he
was smart he would use that reaction, make it work for
him, not against him. He still wanted Sara. So did
Cruzero. If he could get Sara to cooperate, she might
help to lure Cruzero into a trap. Cruzero might con-
fide in her, or he might lose his head and do something stupid. There was lots of potential in this
situation; all he had to do was think it through and
turn the situation to his advantage. All he had to do
was exploit it. That was what he intended to do.

Chapter 3

It was the middle of the workweek when word leaked out from the Miami Police Department that there had been a sensational drug bust. The big story revitalized the doldrum atmosphere in the newsroom. Everyone fervently and silently thanked God.

Walking into the newsroom from the photography department, Sara discovered that Alex's special unit was responsible and that he would be issuing an official statement to the media on behalf of the Narcotics Division. The city editor wanted Sara and their most seasoned reporter, Herb Olsen, to cover the event. Herb was up for a Pulitzer prize in general reporting.

When they arrived, they found the police holding warehouse heavily guarded and crawling with newspaper and television crews. The drug bust was a media event because a prominent rancher involved in state politics was implicated; he had allowed the Dade

County drug runners to use the landing strip on his sprawling ranch. Sara and Herb elbowed their way through the melee, flashing their press cards at guards. Inside the warehouse the cocaine and the money were lined up in neat stacks and rows. The clicks of cameras and a galaxy of flashbulbs filled the air as the journalists converged on the mind-boggling haul. Reporters from the local newspapers and TV crews from the local stations shoved and pushed to get closer, jockeying for position. It was utter chaos.

"My God—look at that money! What I wouldn't give for just one little stack added to my salary." Herb shook his silvered head, laughing to himself while he made copious notes.

"I never knew this much money existed. When it's stacked three feet high in front of you, it's staggering, but somehow becomes meaningless," Sara said, lining up the stacks in her viewfinder and getting to work.

When she had taken enough shots of the money, she concentrated on the narcotic detectives involved in the arrest, who were standing around while Herb grilled them for names and details.

"Where on the plane was the money found? What kind of plane was it? How many people were taken into custody? What are their names?" He fired a succession of staccato questions at one of the detectives while reporters around them fired similar ones at others. But they weren't having much success.

"Lieutenant Cordera, head of Centac, will make a statement any minute now. He'll answer your questions." Mike Garcia smiled and fobbed them off good-naturedly.

Sara recognized the detective instantly. His comments about Alex made her gaze flick restlessly around. The broad-shouldered back of a tall man in a deep blue suit who had paused to talk to two men riveted her attention. The proud bearing, the thick dark hair worn a little on the long side, grazing the crisp shirt collar, identified him instantly. Alex's clothes were one of his weaknesses; he looked like a man who wore only the best. Women's heads turned whenever he walked into a room and other men inevitably asked who his tailor was. The truth was he bought his suits off the peg and looked just as good half-naked.

Everyone waited. In a matter of moments he would be making his official statement to the media. Finished with whatever he had to say, Alex swung around. Dignified, serious, his facial expression and manner coolly professional, he began to read the prepared statement. Focusing on her job, Sara tried to forget that the man she was lining up in the viewfinder was someone she had been married to briefly, was someone she had been intimate with, was someone who had grabbed her in a parking lot only a few nights ago. His slightly accented voice fed the journalists with the details they craved and devoured avariciously. Even engulfed in the crowd Sara felt the searing effect of his authoritative, impressive presence taking its toll on her composure.

For a moment she paused in wonderment. Could this coolly professional, dignified detective possibly be the same man who had grabbed her, hauled her up against a brick wall in a parking lot and then shouted inflammatory things in her ears? The humiliating act he had perpetrated seemed illusory. For a dizzying moment she thought she had somehow imagined the whole thing.

While the low-pitched Cuban rumble rolled around the room with its flowing rhythmic tones, Sara watched Alex scan the assembled press. Flashbulbs zapped, going off like a firework display. Alex and his men had made one of the biggest busts in the county, but everybody standing there knew that it was just a drop in the endless flood of cocaine that flowed into the country, some twenty tons of it every year. What made this cocaine seizure newsworthy was the people involved and the size of the shipment; otherwise it would have been relegated to three or four inches in the back pages of the newspapers.

When he finished reading the official police statement, which gave a minimum of detail, Alex signaled that it was time for questions. The barrage began.

"Is your principal informant in this investigation a former drug runner who used the airstrip himself?"

"He is. Whenever possible we pit criminal against criminal," Alex answered. "We get that to work for us."

"Was the airstrip of this ranch being used over a long period of time for cocaine shipments? How much cocaine would you say came in through this landing strip?"

"To the best of our knowledge it has been in operation for several years. We estimate something like fifteen million dollars' worth of contraband has entered through it."

"How did you stumble onto the Dade County ring?"

"Their pilots kept crashing," Alex fired back, smiling widely. "We got lucky."

Leaning against the wall adjusting the lens on her camera, Sara looked up from the viewfinder as a reporter standing next to her shouted, "How much money was the airstrip's owner getting every time a plane landed?"

"They were charging up to $100,000 per load," Alex responded. Then the force of his gaze locked onto Sara's for an instant. She knew he had seen her, but his facial expression hadn't changed.

On the job Alex was pure cop. Nothing else mattered, nothing else got in the way. Swallowed up by the crowd, Sara was just another bothersome member of the media, someone to brush away like a pesky mosquito. Playing a charade that fooled everyone but themselves, both of them highly tuned in to the other's presence, they continued to ignore each other. But Sara knew Alex had been on her mind for weeks. The impact of the night outside the bar hadn't faded. Branded by the burning anger, the reawakened emotions mingled with desire she had seen in his eyes, she hadn't been able to shake it off.

Having answered his quota of questions, and ignoring any further ones, Alex made his way through the crush and exited the building.

Alex strode toward his car, but he didn't get into it. Leaning against the side of it, he lit a cigarette and watched as Sara emerged from the building with the crowd. Over the burning tip he saw her walk toward her car with Herb Olsen. Alex knew many of the journalists on a first-name basis. He stood watching

his ex-wife talking to Olsen; they enjoyed an easy rapport. Seeing her in the crowd in his own milieu,
knowing that he was going to run into her again and
again, only fueled his desire to go after what he
wanted. His resolve hardened.

Since the night at the Country and Western Tavern
his plan had taken shape. He wanted to accomplish
two things where Sara was concerned: he wanted to
start seeing her again, and he wanted to warn her
about Raphael Cruzero, to see if he could get her on
his side, get her to cooperate with him to nail Cruzero. To accomplish the first objective he had somehow to smooth things over between them.

His mind flashed back to the parking lot outside the
bar. He had lost his head, his temper, his control, and
he had gotten more than a little rough. Smoothing
things over wasn't going to be easy. But he was putting his money on that unequivocal response he had
felt in her, the way her quivering flesh molded to his,
the way her lips had softened and yielded under his for
a fleeting moment, the way she had pressed her face
into his neck, so that he couldn't see her fighting her
own desire. He was going to have to play it cool—if a
Cuban with a fiery temperament, a lot of smoldering
resentment and the hots for his ex-wife could ever play
it cool, he thought, amused at himself. He sure as hell
meant to find out.

When Sara came out of the newsroom the following day, Alex was lounging against the wall near the
elevators, waiting for her. She didn't see him at first.
One of the younger reporters, Jack Paterson, had exited the newsroom beside her, and regaling her with an

anecdote about a drug bust he had covered. The drug trafficking business was all new territory to Sara and fascinated her. She listened with rapt attention to the reporter—who was also angling for a date. But when she saw Alex she stopped dead in her tracks.

Alex's burning gaze sent her a silent message. The young reporter glanced around speculatively to see what the distraction was, then appeared openly irritated when he recognized Alex standing there, looking as if he wanted to eat Sara alive. Sara excused herself, not taking the guy up on his offer of an evening out. After summing up his tale with a few glib remarks, Jack tossed her a friendly farewell, saying he had a deadline to meet.

For a moment Sara paused uncertainly, then avoided the bank of elevators where Alex waited and headed for the stairs. Alex easily caught up with her and trapped her on the stairwell. When she tried to go past he barred her way.

"What are you doing here?"

"I want to talk to you." They stared at each other for a long tense moment.

"For someone who claims to have lost a vital part of his anatomy you've got an awful lot of nerve."

Alex smiled with wicked roguish charm and his eyes danced. "I said that was how you made me feel. I never said you succeeded, Sara. Big difference."

"I don't think we have anything to talk about." She flashed him a cold smile. Some people walked around them on the stairs. "I wish you would leave me alone. I've got work to do, assignments to finish, deadlines to meet."

"This will only take a few minutes." His darkening eyes drilled into her. "Come with me. I have to talk to you."

"I don't want to go *anywhere* with you. I don't want to be *alone* with you." She started down the stairs again, but his arm and body barred the way. He angled his head downward, so that he was looking into her eyes.

"Sara, I want to apologize for my behavior at the Country and Western Tavern. Will you accept my apology?"

Measuring the truth of what he said, she ignored two more people darting past them. His gaze followed them for a moment, then he turned back to her. "Isn't there somewhere better we can talk?"

Without a word she started back up the stairs. He followed her. She led him down the corridor past the newsroom to a small lounge used for coffee breaks. At this time of day the lounge was vacant.

Alex towered over her, looking darkly magnetic and somehow completely unrepentant for what had happened between them. But he sounded sincere when he said, "I lost my head and I got rough with you. For that I'm truly sorry. Will you accept my apology?"

Lowering her gaze, she searched her mind, then put her thoughts into words. "What do you want from me? Why are you here?"

"Sara, I'm sorry." His smile asked if that was so hard to believe. "I made an ass out of myself. I am one volatile Latino. I acted like an . . . overheated primate. You agree with me, don't you, on that much?" He raised an eyebrow at her.

"For once we are in complete agreement. This amazes me," she remarked, unable to suppress a smile.

"Me too," he said dryly. "We also both have to live and work in Miami. Our work overlaps. We're going to keep on running into each other. Doesn't it make sense for us to smooth things over? I want us to do that. It would make me happy if we could do that."

Charming when he used that soft tone of intimacy and humor, he could work magic. When he was like this Alex was hard to refuse. Besides, what he was saying made sense. They would be running into each other. She closed her eyes, for a moment feeling herself yielding. "All right, I accept your apology."

Like fine old cognac his lazy smiling regard continued to warm her. "You know something, Sara? That incident could have been avoided if we had met and talked things over. The way we met again, we took each other by storm, got off on the wrong foot. Why don't you let me take you out to dinner? Isn't it time we talked things over?"

She hesitated, wondering what they might achieve.

Not allowing the opportunity to slide by, Alex seized it and wrapped it up. "There's something else we have to talk about—your friend Raphael Cruzero. I'd like you to come to my office. There's something I want to show you."

Intrigued, Sara searched his eyes, her own full of questions. "What would you be able to tell me about Raphael? What would you have there to show me?"

"Come to my office after work tomorrow and you'll find out. Then I'll take you out to dinner. We can talk. This time we can talk calmly about some things we should have talked about seven years ago.''

Before she could think of any arguments or obstacles to put in his way, he turned and strode out into the hall, leaving her staring at him. With a strange sense of defeat she leaned against the side of the vending machine, trying to regain her composure. Suddenly she realized she hadn't answered him. She didn't have to. He knew she would be there.

Leaving the imposing *Miami Guardian* building behind her, Sara hurried toward the parking lot. She was running late. Since Alex had mentioned going out to dinner, she had rushed to the rest room after work to change her clothes. Now she was wearing a yellow dress with a wide belt that flattered her waist and called attention to the curve of her hips.

Luckily it wasn't far to the Miami Police Department but heavy traffic made the drive seem longer than it was.

She was still slightly breathless and a little exasperated when the elevator doors slid back at the second floor, revealing the huge area that was the Narcotics Division. Fluorescent lighting in long strips illuminated row after row of desks and computer terminals, a silent testimony to the war on drugs. Because of the time, most of the desks had been abandoned. Only a few diehards remained working late. Along the sides were partitioned glassed-in offices. She was scanning the offices, wondering which belonged to Alex, when a tall figure emerged from one several doors down.

Tall and broad-shouldered, Alex was even more impressive without a jacket. With a shoulder holster strapped diagonally across his torso, his macho brand of uncompromising masculinity was reinforced. The dark Hispanic complexion contrasted with the light-colored dress shirt, open at the collar, his tie loosened. His expression told her it had been a long day.

Whether she liked it or not, she knew Alex was not just hovering around the edges of her life; soon he would be trying to force his way back in.

He spoke as soon as he saw her. "I thought maybe you wouldn't come, after all. Did you have any trouble finding it?"

"No trouble," she murmured, stepping in front of him when he opened the door to his office. For a moment their body heat and scents intermingled, bringing a heady intimacy. Images of the past flashed mercilessly through her mind—the same images that had been tormenting her over and over again in the night, dizzying memories of passion.

Inside his office she turned slowly around, surveying the room. She searched for a safe topic to open a conversation between them. On the wall behind his desk she found the perfect thing—an impressive-looking plaque. Walking over to it she perused the plaque silently, then read the inscription aloud.

"DRUG
ENFORCEMENT ADMINISTRATION
United States
Department of Justice
Presents
This Certificate of
Appreciation
to

Alex Cordera
for
Outstanding Contributions
in the Field of Drug
Law Enforcement"

She turned back to Alex, smiling. "I'm very impressed."

"I always like to impress the ladies." The Cuban charm asserted itself immediately; flirting was second nature to him.

His eyes drilled into her. "But I didn't impress you enough to keep you."

"I told you why I left. It wasn't because I didn't find you impressive. Believe me, I always found you impressive in every situation." They studied each other for a moment, then Sara turned away, scanning the other furnishings and trying to get back on safe ground. With a leisurely movement she looked back to him, focusing her eyes on his face.

"Well, you got me here. Now what is it you want?"

"I always cared what happened to you," he announced. "I still care what happens to you. That's why I wanted you in here. That's why I'm showing you this file on Raphael."

His charm suddenly evaporated. Ruthless professionalism took its place. He snapped up a folder from his desk and thrust it at her. "Read it, Sara."

The clipped soft command echoed in the stillness of his office. She sat down, opened the folder and focused her attention on the contents, trying to forget its source. But she was acutely aware of him leaning against the desk, knowing full well his eyes were burning holes in her clothes.

Sara read the file. She was stunned, barely aware that Alex had moved behind her chair. In the opinion of the police Raphael Cruzero was deeply involved with people known to be actively engaged in drug trafficking. They suspected he had moved high on the corporate ladder of the Cali cartel, which was the driving force behind several blind trusts and shell corporations set up in Panama and the Cayman Islands. These were highly suspect operations, the type often set up to launder large sums of drug money. At the present time Raphael appeared to be engaged in legitimate business, owning a string of car dealerships in Miami, prime real estate, shopping malls and condominiums scattered around the city. His family had always been affluent in Colombia, Sara thought to herself, but nothing like this! After a long silence she slowly closed the folder and finally found her voice.

"Have you got any evidence that will stand up in court?"

"Not yet. But we will. We're going to nail him, Sara. That's why I don't want to see you mixed up with him. I was hoping you would cooperate with us in some way."

Looking up at him, she replied softly, "But in this country a man is innocent until proved guilty. I can't believe the man described in this folder is the Raphael Cruzero *I know,* even if he fits the division's profile of a high-level drug trafficker. What possible reason could he have for getting involved in anything like this? He was already wealthy. He comes from a good family. None of this makes any sense to me—even if it were true—which I refuse to believe it is."

Alex still stood behind her. He leaned down to her, his soft accented voice rolling into her ear. "Raphael is the kind of guy who would always want ten dollars if he had only five. Greed doesn't make a lot of sense, Sara. There's only one way you can figure it out."

"What's that?"

"The more you get the more you want. That's true of some other things I can think of." The message clicked into her mind as he intended. When she looked at him, Alex's lazy eyes darkened and the charismatic smile deepened the corners of his mouth. A heavy sensuality thickened between them, drugging her mind. Her lips struggled to form words. Her gaze dropped. Finally she managed to speak.

"Suspicion isn't good enough for me, Alex. Not when it comes to an old friend like Raphael. I don't accept it now and I never will," she murmured. She watched a telltale muscle flex in his jaw as his tanned fingers gripped her own jaw, forcing her to look straight into his eyes. When Alex was ticked off his eyes became hard, flat, compelling stones.

"Listen to me, Sara. And listen good. Eventually we will prove our suspicions. But these things take time. It's very difficult to prove conspiracy to deal in drugs, to build a case against someone who may never go within a mile of the 'merchandise.' What we as investigators need is *prior* knowledge. We have to rely heavily on informants and even more on the penetration of their operations by undercover detectives. What makes it even more difficult is that drug traffickers are very much aware of the way we work. Colombians have a distinct edge over other traffickers because whenever and wherever possible they employ and deal only with their fellow countrymen. For those reasons Raphael's operation is going to be a hard nut to crack, but we will get him. Don't get involved with him. This could all blow up in your face. You work for a prestigious newspaper. Do you want to risk your job?''

"We're talking about an old friend of my family." Choked emotion surfaced in her words. Somehow when he attacked Raphael, he was attacking her own cherished associations with the past, those happy times spent with her family and his. The desire to keep those happy memories intact made her view what Alex said with scorn, made her blind, in fact. She had looked at the printed words in the folder, but she didn't see; she listened to Alex's warnings, but she didn't hear. "We're talking about loyalty. Not running risks with my job."

"Loyalty is a good thing, Sara . . . as long as it's not misguided. In your case it is." His fingers tightened on her jaw.

"Take your hand away," she murmured. "You're too close. Maybe I should get one of those court restraining orders so that you have to remain at least five feet away from me at all times."

"Restraint never worked for us, remember?" he pointed out in low amused tones.

"I simply refuse to believe what you're saying until there is some conclusive proof and enough of it to take him to court."

Alex let his hand drop, then moved away behind his desk. Placing his hands palms down on the desk he lowered his gaze to hide his reaction to her continued resistance. His unraveling temper spurred on his sharp humor. "You laugh at this profile. But if it acts like a duck and looks like a duck and sounds like a duck, what the hell is it, Sara? The Narcotics Division doesn't act capriciously. We don't pick on people, single out certain people on a whim." He emphasized his point by rapping the table twice with his index finger and looking straight a her.

"We don't reason the same way, Alex."

"So I discovered seven years ago." He laughed dryly.

She rose from the chair and shoved the file back at him in retaliation. He was never going to let her forget the past; it kept cropping up in everything he did and said. When she continued to stare at him, he eased off.

He closed his eyes, smiling that smile that wasn't a smile at all, that only covered up growing irritation and other feelings. Easing off was just a ploy to throw her off guard momentarily, she knew. Alex never backed off anything.

"All right, Sara. I've been patiently explaining to you and getting nowhere. This conversation is at an end." He rapped his finger against the table again with rhythmic sharpness, but more emphatically this time. Slowly straightening, he adjusted his tie. He picked up his jacket from the back of the desk chair and shrugged into it. "We have a table waiting for us." Holding the office door open, he looked down at her, lazy sensuality returning to his eyes. "You will want to have dinner with me, don't you?"

"Why not? I've got nothing better to do and I am very hungry."

"So am I, Sara."

His explicit look silenced her. They walked slowly toward the elevator. Alex's undisguised interest unnerved her, but made her feel intensely female. Other men never made her feel the way he did, at least not to the same degree. That feeling was seductive, heady and intoxicating, and she knew from experience she could get emotionally high on it. But the way Alex made a woman feel demanded a high price. He not only expected a lot; he took a lot for granted. Sacrifices had to be made to be his kind of woman. At nineteen she had not wanted to pay the price. She was even more sure she didn't want to pay it now. But Alex had a look in his eye that suggested his mind was not working in the same direction hers was.

Alive with the sound of voices, laughter and the clink of cutlery and glassware, the restaurant was jammed. They made their way through the closely set tables, harried waiters rushing past them. Alex guided Sara to a paneled booth in a corner. A waiter walked up to confirm their reservation and place menus on the table, which he then pulled out so Sara could slide in. Alex slowly sank down next to her.

Turning lazily, he looked sideways at her, but his darkening eyes reflected purpose. She realized Raphael was still on his mind. He hadn't given up yet. Even though she had told him how she felt, she knew he was still going to try to sway her.

"If you won't give me your cooperation, Sara, I hope you have enough sense to remember what I said and stay away from him."

"You don't like Raphael very much, do you? I'm beginning to wonder if there isn't some kind of personal vendetta here. Why do I have the feeling I've walked into the middle of something?"

"Because you have, Sara—when you walked back into my life."

He leaned forward, hunching the impressive line of his shoulders, resting his forearms on the table. A pin-striped shirt and deep blue silk tie the same color as his suit complemented his dark good looks and the sensuality of his features. His burnt sienna eyes looked absolutely unmovable, very serious, slightly dangerous and very streetwise. He examined her with them. Controlling the woman in front of him was his main objective, she knew, and he wasn't having much success. It was clear that his Latin temperament was already on a very short fuse.

"I would never go after a man purely because of a personal vendetta. People who get involved in drug trafficking are merchants of misery, Sara. That's why I'm after him, not for any personal reasons. I want your cooperation, not your hostility."

She wasn't so sure about that.

"I'm not nineteen anymore. I'll make up my own mind about Raphael. You can't issue orders, tell me what I can and can't do."

He swore softly, turning his head to the side to let out a long string of Spanish expletives. "So that's it. We're getting back to that. Is that why you ran out on me? Is that how you remember things between us—*me* telling you what to do? You were nineteen and pregnant. You needed someone to tell you what to do. You left me no choice." His finger rapped the table. He regarded her with an autocratic look that said as always he was very sure of his actions.

"I thought we came here to talk things over calmly."

"We are talking things over calmly. Why the hell did you leave me a lousy four-line note?" he snapped.

"For the very reason you're demonstrating right now. You're arrogant, impossibly macho, cocksure of yourself. You would have tried to stop me."

"You're right, I would have tried to stop you. You were my wife. I had every right. That's supposed to mean something, even today."

The waiter arrived. They both looked up and stared at him, his presence an intrusion. He took their orders, then disappeared. Alex leaned back again with an expression that said he wasn't finished.

He flicked an amused eyebrow at her. "Remember how we met?"

"I remember." A soft smile that she couldn't suppress crept onto her face.

"That first night I met you you looked at least twenty-three or twenty-four to me. That look in your eyes said you were experienced, that you knew what you were doing. But you didn't know. And you didn't do anything to correct my wrong impression. Do you realize what I'm saying?"

"I suppose you're trying to say that it was mostly my fault. If I hadn't let you think I was older, more experienced, you would have left me alone, walked away."

"No, Sara. The blame rests with me more than you. I knew what I was doing. When I found out how young you were, I knew I should walk away, but I couldn't keep my hands off you." He studied his hands resting on the table.

Avoiding his eyes, she responded slowly. "All I can remember is, after we were married you always looked like you were doing some kind of slow burn. I thought you were blaming me."

He leaned his impressive frame forward and rested his arms on the tablecloth again. His darkening eyes raked her face. "Every night when I got back to the condo I was reminded of how young you were."

It was clear they both felt some remorse over their reckless behavior.

"You were impossibly macho and arrogant about everything in those days. I remember feeling as if I couldn't talk to you about anything. Least of all my feelings. And you're still the same. I'm not nineteen now, but you still seem the same. You're still trying to tell me what to do. How do you explain that? Not five minutes ago you told me to stay away from an old friend."

"That's different."

"Is it?"

He paused for only a brief moment. "Why didn't you ever say anything to me about any of this? Why didn't you explain the way you felt in a letter or with a phone call after you left?"

"I don't know. I thought it was over and done with, why stir it all up again?"

Alex regarded her. She thought she saw a tension developing in his manner. It made her uneasy. Her gaze slid to the deepening grooves on either side of his mouth.

"If we were in the same situation all over again, what would you do now? Would you do anything differently?"

"That's a hypothetical question."

"I know, but I want you to answer it."

"In the same situation, given the same conditions, I would probably do the same thing all over again. I wouldn't want to spend my life with someone who was only with me because it was the right thing to do." The look in his eyes fried her nerve endings as the lines around his mouth deepened with amusement. There was also a hardening about him, as if he was confirming something in his own mind, telling himself something, cautioning himself somehow.

"Well, it's all water under the bridge now," she said. "Hypothetical questions are a waste of time."

"Sometimes they're not," he retorted enigmatically. "I keep asking myself that question. What happened the other night between us? Why did it happen? Have you answered that question in your mind yet?" The deceptively amiable smile did not reach the burning intensity of his eyes. Suddenly, a dismissive look glazed his eyes. Glancing upward to see why, she saw the waiter approach their table, setting down a heavy tray. With a flourish he put the steaming serving dishes on the table, then disappeared. Alex surveyed the contents, then passed one or two to her, afterward helping himself without a word. The look of absorption in his eyes told her he was thinking.

"I came here to smooth things over," she said softly. "I want to forget what happened that night. It's over now.'' With a look in her eyes she underlined what she meant.

"I think you're kidding yourself." He returned her look with one of his own, then cut into the prime rib.

The implication behind his words—that it wasn't over between them—left her feeling uneasy. She didn't want what he had in mind, what was going to happen next. They sat in an awkward silence, neither one able to think of a thing to say.

After the waiter arrived some time later with coffee, they sat watching each other in wary silence as they drank it. When Alex asked Sara a few questions about her job, she realized it was an attempt to get away from the volatile subject of their past and the equally volatile subject of Raphael Cruzero. They talked of inconsequential things, but acted restless with each other until he checked his watch and announced it was time to leave.

When they left the restaurant the balmy night held an aura of pervasive sensuality heavy with the scent of jasmine. A strong sensation of déjà vu attacked her. As they walked to the car, the same sensations that had swept over her seven years ago were doing so now. Her ex-husband was sensual and emotional dynamite and she was still looking for love. The basic urge to mate, to find a partner for life, was always there, calling and pulling her like some strong undertow, in spite of the fact that she knew Alex was completely unsuitable for her. There was still an irresistible attraction between Alex and her. Whether she wanted it or not, as Alex had already pointed out, there was still a lot going on between them and it wasn't just physical.

"I left my car at the police department," she reminded him, pointedly calling his attention to the fact that she had to get back.

"I know where your car is. Relax." His rapid-fire response had an edge to it.

She looked in the other direction, with a flush of embarrassment. She was acting like some high-strung filly locked into a corral with a stallion that knew she was coming into heat. Alex's knowing eyes were watching for the signs and he hadn't forgotten any of them. Sliding in the passenger side with a sensation of vulnerability hovering around her again, Sara sank back into the bucket seat wondering what he was going to do next. Alex lowered his powerful frame into the other side and started up the engine, popping a cassette into the tape deck. Music filled the car, covering up the smoldering silence between them as he drove with intent absorption back to the Miami Police Department.

As they arrived, she rummaged through her handbag for her keys, but they eluded her. Frustration ate away at her composure as she got out of his car, thumping her clutch bag against the passenger door in silent agitation. She walked quickly to her car. Alex caught up with her.

"Sara?"

The softly spoken words demanded an answer. She turned around, slowly running a hand through her hair in a distracted way. He planted himself between her and the car door. She had to think quickly and stop what was threatening to happen between them. What better way to halt it than to declare that they be "good friends"?

"You know, Alex, I'm really glad that we've smoothed things over. It was a good idea, having dinner and talking things over. We can be friends from now on." She smiled at him, but the smile wavered slightly. Wanting to put an end to all this sexual tension building between them, she was bargaining for release from it with her eyes. He leaned back against the side of her car. Spreading his legs slightly, he reached out and pulled her into his arms. Alex was sure of himself and sure of what he wanted and how to get it, and it was the look in his eyes that was doing all the talking.

"We can never be friends. You know that and I know that." His hand reached out to the curve of her neck, pulling her close so that only inches separated his face from hers. She reached up a hand to dislodge his hold on her, then clung to his wrist when he wouldn't let go.

"What do you mean we can never be friends?" she demanded softly. "That's what this whole evening was about, to talk over the past, to smooth things over. I didn't have dinner with you tonight so that we could remain enemies."

"We're not enemies, either. We both know that, too."

His husky tone and the look in his eyes were already telling her that he had no intention of listening to anything she said.

He wasted no time following up his intentions. Lowering his head and pressing his mouth against hers he breathed against her lips, "You want me to show you why we can never be friends?" With ruthless domination his mouth closed over hers. One hand roughly grazed the side of her jaw. Then, he cupped her face with his hands, his eyes meeting hers with his silent message. Her lips answered the warm intoxicating pressure of his, so different from the humiliating kisses of their last encounter. When he broke off the initial foray, Sara rested her hands on his shoulders near his neck and turned her head to the side. Lean, hard fingers locked on her jaw.

"I never could keep my hands off you, Sara, could I? I never could get enough." Hot and quick, his words of explanation flowed into her ears and fanned her lips. "I don't feel like this around a friend, Sara. Believe me when I tell you that."

She shifted in his arms, her growing agitation only fueling his escalating excitement and his confidence. He knew the way he disturbed her was equal to the way she disturbed him. He used it, exploited it to its fullest. Basking in the solid warmth of him, clinging to something she had lost long ago, she permitted his mouth to capture hers again. The sensual magic he wielded came back in full force. Tonight he had seduction on his mind, not humiliation. She knew he was out to make a valid statement about the way they still affected each other. Their lips mated hungrily, their kisses deepening as he drew her slowly against the hard line of his thighs. The thin material of her dress couldn't mask the undeniable arousal building between them. The ache for a fulfillment of a love lost seven years ago, cut off before its full flower had developed, drove her hands upward. Her fingers locked around the corded flesh of his neck. Forcing her in to him with a sudden compulsive urge, he covered her face with a rough, fiery succession of kisses.

Chapter 4

Raphael's Aston Martin slowed down at the docks. He leaped out of the car, then helped Sara slide out. His dark wavy hair, broad features and flashy good looks were enhanced by a white dinner jacket. For a moment he and Sara gazed at the yacht about two hundred yards away. It was festooned with lights, lying on the dark waters of the bay. The low roar of voices and laughter mingled with Latin American music hung on the humid night air.

As a speedboat ferried Sara and Raphael from the dock to the yacht, she was aware of Raphael taking in her windblown blond curls and the classic simplicity of her strapless black evening gown.

On deck they were soon caught up in the crush of people. The midnight cruise on the 150-foot floating palace was an invitation no one in Miami wanted to turn down. When Raphael had telephoned to invite

"You still like my hands on you. Nothing's changed that, has it, Sara?"

"No." She breathed the reply without thinking before his mouth captured hers again. When he broke off the heated exchange, his hot breath fanned the soft skin of her neck.

"I know you want me, Sara, the same way I knew it seven years ago." His words trailed over the shell of her ear. Still holding her locked against him, he moved his hand under her full skirt until it reached her thighs, then let both hands wander over her buttocks. Kissing her again and again, he repeated her name between each heated kiss.

"Sara...Sara...Sara." He was becoming deeply aroused. Pushing himself into the soft curves of her womanhood, he continued repeating her name with mind-drugging effect. She pressed her forehead against his, breathed his name softly against his questing lips, shuddered with awakening desire. Then raw urgency clawed them both. Alex's breathing altered; his hands clamped down hard on her hips, demanding satisfaction. He made a low animallike sound in his throat, then it escaped from his lips.

This sudden rush of mounting desire alarmed her as nothing else could, bringing her to her senses. Regaining control, she suddenly pulled away, as if she had touched something too hot. She drew the back of her hand to her lips.

Alex gazed down at her with equal amounts of naked desire and male aggression mingling in his eyes. "Come back to my place with me. This is how it is between us."

She looked into his intense eyes, rea[...] didn't know this man; she had never [...] him. Everything about him alarmed he[...] was overwhelmed by everything he did a[...]

"Sara, I want you, you want me. Did y[...] I said?"

She shook her head silently. "We can't [...] all over again. We hurt each other once. [...] stincts tell me it's going to happen again[...] time I have the feeling it will be worse tha[...] time." Her eyes searched his. "The warning [...] going off in my head. Why aren't they goi[...] yours?"

"Maybe I don't want to hear them," he fi[...] quietly.

her a week ago, he explained that the gala evening was to promote the annual offshore powerboat races.

"Half of Miami is here, I think," he murmured now in her ear. People clogged the passageways, spilling out of salons. Infectious, upbeat merengue music pulsed through the human melange. Sporadic laughter erupted around them. Many women wore designer originals, set off by jewels that caught fire in the evening lights. As Raphael led Sara through the press of people, a raised voice caught their attention.

"Raphael, my good friend!" A man of medium build, sporting a white dinner jacket, a black T-shirt, tuxedo pants and tennis shoes hailed them, then walked toward them. His flamboyant attire suggested an equally flamboyant personality. "I'm so glad you could both come to my party," he announced when he drew near. He was not very tall, and he had the affable relaxed charm of a man who never had to worry where his next two or three hundred thousand was coming from. "Who is this beautiful young woman, Raphael? Where have you been hiding her?"

Raphael turned immediately to Sara to make the introduction. "Sara, may I present my good friend Carlos Ramirez. Carlos, this is my good friend Sara Langston. She's a photographer for the *Miami Guardian* but she used to work for *World Photographic.*"

Carlos Ramirez nodded his head deferentially. "I am pleased to meet you. Beauty and intelligence is an irresistible combination and one that is not all that common." The old-world gallantry suggested that, like Raphael, he was Colombian.

"I hope you will have a good time. Cruising up the Intracoastal Waterway on a night like this will make it impossible not to have a good time. And it is also in aid of a very good cause." He mentioned a well-known charity.

"Everyone in Miami has been talking about it for weeks," she responded warmly.

"*Gracias.* I hope that it lives up to your expectations. I want you both to enjoy yourselves." He politely remarked to Sara, "*Y con permiso,* later I want to discuss some business with Raphael. I promise that I will keep him for only fifteen minutes or so."

She smiled agreeably.

"I'll get back to you both in a little while. Meanwhile enjoy yourselves." He propelled them in the general direction of the main salon where there was food and drink, then excused himself.

Raphael's arm closed around her waist. "How do you know him?" she asked idly.

"He is Colombian. I knew his family in Bogotá. His father exports emeralds. He came to Miami and I met him again through my real estate dealings. We're buying some property together. Negotiations are ongoing and I have to talk to him later for a few minutes. It won't take long, I promise," he reassured with a deepening smile. He turned in the general direction of the bar. "Something to drink? Champagne?"

At Sara's nod he disappeared into the crowd. She leaned back against the side of the deck, looking around. There was a sharp blast, and she saw crew members beginning to cast off. Raphael returned in a few minutes with a drink for himself and a crystal flute of champagne for her.

"Where exactly are we going?" she inquired over the rim of the glass.

"Up the Intracoastal Waterway to Lake Worth and back. It's a nice cruise for evening," he announced. "It will take several hours."

Sara raked her wind-tossed hair away from her face. Looking around, she recognized a few local celebrities, and between the dancing couples she caught a glimpse of the Latin American band playing on the aft deck. She relaxed and enjoyed the balmy evening breeze as she listened to the music, which had slowed from a frenetic merengue to a romantic ballad.

"It's so beautiful, so tranquil," she remarked, gazing out over the water.

"Very beautiful," he murmured when she turned back to face him. The compliment in his eyes told her it was not the scenery that occupied his mind. Her mind chose that moment to remind her of Alex's warnings about Raphael. Though she still rejected the possibility that her old friend was actively engaged in drug trafficking, she believed it possible that he might conceivably have business contacts with fellow countrymen who were—and that he might not appreciate how risky they were. Any association with that kind of people was playing with fire. Out of loyalty she wanted to warn him, to make him aware that some people had taken notice and were watching him closely.

He rested his forearms on the side of the yacht, gazing at the dark water churning below. "That look in your eyes tells me something is bothering you, Sara. You have been different toward me. Something is wrong. What is it?" he demanded quietly, reaching into his pocket for one of his beloved cheroots.

Because she knew that her remarks would be bound to disturb him, she didn't answer right away. She had to choose her words carefully. Looking at him, wanting to speak but not wanting to offend or hurt him, she still hesitated.

"What is it, Sara?" Watching her, he lit the cheroot. For a moment her gaze dropped to his heavy gold lighter, a square-cut emerald adorning it.

"Through a contact in the newsroom, a confidential source, I heard something...disturbing about you." Not wanting to increase the enmity she knew already existed between the two men, she didn't mention Alex's name.

Raphael reached out his hand, pushing away the curling blond tendril from the flare of her cheekbone. Then his hand dropped to the curve of her neck, resting there. "What did someone tell you, Sara?" The look of possession was in his eyes, mixed with wariness.

"This confidential source said that you associated with—" she hated to use the term, but there was no other way around it "—with people involved in drug trafficking," she finished lamely, feeling like some kind of Judas.

He looked at her with a perceptive glimmer in his eyes. Then, without hesitation, he responded to her question. "Sara, I have a chain of car dealerships. I own prime real estate, condominiums, a couple of shopping malls. Do you think I can check out the source of the wealth of every man I do business with, the source of all his currency?" He shrugged. "I have to live in this less than perfect world. I am a businessman. I have to survive. It's impossible to do business in Miami and not come into contact directly or indirectly with drug money."

She stared at him steadily, trying to measure what he was saying. "Are you saying that from time to time that you do business with them unwittingly, or are you saying that you do business with them knowingly and simply turn a blind eye to their source of income?"

"These people who traffic in drugs are a fact of life. If I don't do business with them, someone else will. More importantly, if I don't do business with them, some of my fellow countrymen might take offense. There is always the possibility of harsh reprisals from Colombians here or back in Colombia to members of my family. I do not want to be found floating facedown in the Miami River." His dark eyes were lazy with roguish amusement.

The explanation was that he had little choice whether he wanted to or not. Raphael was no fool. Underneath his charm he was as sharp as a whip. Inventive, ambitious and imaginative, he had always possessed these qualities. From the time they were young Raphael had displayed a marked ability to organize any activity, to turn a situation to his advantage. When it came to a challenging contest of any kind he always stood out. If asked, she would have said that he channeled these energies into acceptable outlets, that they helped to make him the successful entrepreneur that he was. For a moment she wondered just how far he would go, if he set limits for himself, guidelines.

"Raphael—the confidential source mentioned a file."

He searched her eyes, measuring her words. "As a businessman I have to report all cash sales over ten thousand dollars. Maybe that is why some government department keeps a file on me."

"It also mentioned shell corporations in the Cayman Islands and the Bahamas."

His eyes gleamed with amusement. "I have some blind trusts set up, to avoid taxes. This is a perfectly legitimate business practice."

She felt relieved, but couldn't resist one more query. "You would never get *directly* involved with any of these people knowingly, would you? You wouldn't risk everything, your good name, all that you come from, out of sheer greed?" There was a silent plea in her eyes that begged him to give her the answer she longed to hear. It was a naive, almost childish thing to ask, but she wanted it so much she was blinded by the desire.

"Sara," he whispered urgently, taking her face between his hands. "I have a weakness for very beautiful and expensive things, and I enjoy an affluent lifestyle, but that is not a crime. This confidential source I would like to get my hands on." His eyes narrowed shrewdly on her face with a waiting expression that said he wanted her trust, wanted her to confirm that he had it.

"I'm sorry I brought this up. *No importa,*" she murmured.

"*Sí, es muy importante, querida.*"

Her line of questioning showed distrust and doubt. Now there was pain in his eyes. She dropped her gaze, knowing she had wounded him deeply. Guilt surged inside her. She should never have asked in the first place. Why should she doubt the word of an old and trusted friend because of some dubious profile in a folder? Raphael was a friend whose family her own family had been close to, and nothing had been proved against him. That folder had been compiled on suspicion and, like hearsay, would never stand up in a court of law.

She looked away at the passing scene. "Let's forget I ever brought up the subject," she pleaded on an apologetic note. "I don't want anything to spoil a night like this one. It's so beautiful."

Raphael's face relaxed into one of his familiar broad smiles. The pain disappeared from his eyes, warmth returning. "This is a night meant for—"

A voice interrupted him. Carlos, the owner of the yacht, was calling to them.

"Come with me. This will only take a few minutes," Raphael murmured in her ear.

Still feeling like the lowest thing on earth for even raising the subject, she followed in the direction he led. The memory of Alex leaning against his desk in his office, shoving the file at her, macho and cocksure of himself as usual, filled her with bitter resentment. She and Raphael approached the aft deck, where she saw two other men waiting.

Immediately Raphael became involved in an avid business discussion on some last-minute changes in a real estate deal. While he and Carlos rattled on at each other in their native tongue, Sara was left to her own devices. She scanned the guests until she caught sight of some editors she knew from the newspaper. She whispered in Raphael's ear that she was going over to say hello.

He nodded agreeably enough but caught her arm and bent his head, staying her for a moment. "Come back to me. Don't stay too long."

She left his side to join a small enclave of people from the *Miami Guardian*.

"Everyone in Miami who is somebody is here, I think," Michelle Langley, a features writer, announced in impressed tones. "Local politicians, TV personalities, a couple of senators, even an ex-governor. There are some rising stars from the Miami Police Department, too," she said, laughing. "Look over there, Sara—remember that last cocaine seizure you photographed in the police holding warehouse? Isn't that the man who was in charge of the investigation?"

Turning in the direction Michelle indicated, Sara was stunned to see Alex. "He's probably here because he did some local politician a favor."

With an uncanny sixth sense Alex suddenly turned and his restless gaze swung her way. She hadn't had any contact with him since the night they had dinner together to smooth over the past, the same evening that had only served to stir things up even more between them. Now, wanting the predictable effect of his presence to begin to assert itself, she turned abruptly away when his gaze locked onto hers.

The features writer had seen the charged look the two exchanged. "You know each other well?" she fished.

"No, I wouldn't say that."

"That look in his eyes makes a liar out of you. I wouldn't mind if he would look at me like that."

A faint smile played around Sara's mouth. "He looks at all women that way," she said with airy dismissiveness.

They stood talking for a few more minutes until Sara excused herself, with the intention of rejoining Raphael. Some people moved out of her way and suddenly Alex emerged out of nowhere and stepped in front of her. He caught hold of her arm. His Cuban temper was on the boil. His low-pitched staccato words flew at her.

"I give you good advice. Do you follow it? No, that would be too easy for you. Wouldn't it, Sara?" His gaze shifted around restlessly before it returned with exasperation to her face. "Why are you here with him, Sara? Don't you believe anything I told you about him? Don't you think I know how to do my job?"

"When it comes to weighing my loyalty and affection for someone dear to me against the strength of one miserable file, I don't have to tell you which won out."

"That kind of thinking could cost you, Sara, in more ways than one." He fired the words low and quick so that they all ran together.

Unnerved by the fiery explosion in his eyes, she shot back, "That's not all I think. You want to know what else I think?"

He surveyed her, his head tipped to one side in a challenging way. "Go on, tell me."

"I think your obvious dislike of Raphael has distorted your judgment, whether you realize it or not."

"So you think *my* judgment is distorted." He closed his eyes, smiling, savoring the humor in that remark.

"Our past relationship has entered into it."

Alex's eyes turned to steel. His professional conduct was being challenged. He seemed about to issue a sharp retort, but suddenly Raphael's voice sliced through the surrounding gaiety, interrupting them.

Dispensing with any kind of pretense of greeting, Raphael locked his gaze immediately onto Alex. "Sara arrived here with me and she leaves with me. For the rest of the evening stay away from her."

The two men stared fixedly at each other. Raphael had never swallowed Sara's dismissive remarks about there being nothing between her and Alex Cordera, but she was surprised by the naked loathing she saw in their eyes. People all around had picked up on the angry vibrations between the two men. Heads turned. Curious eyes focused on them. The atmosphere was instantly so highly charged that Sara could feel the fine hairs on the back of her neck standing up.

"Raphael, why don't we dance?" she pleaded quietly. For a moment he looked at her and smiled engagingly. But Alex's presence dragged his attention away again. Shifting her firmly out of his way with both hands, Raphael stepped toward Alex.

Sara withdrew to the side of the yacht, leaning back against the railing with an apprehensive air, knowing that fireworks were inevitable. Two fiery, temperamental men at loggerheads—she awaited an explosion of angry words, the hurling of abuse, nothing more. But suddenly, without any warning, Raphael's hand shot out and shoved Alex away from him violently. Alex was caught off balance and fell back against the side of the yacht.

"When she's with me, you stay away. *Comprende!* From now on she is always with me. *Comprende!*"

With stunning reflexes Alex retaliated. Seizing Raphael's lapels he yanked him forward sharply, then slammed him back hard against the railing, reversing their positions. The blinding ferocity of his streaking moves drew loud gasps of amazement. Raphael swung out wildly, the ring on his hand catching the side of Alex's jaw as Alex ducked, and he landed only a glancing blow. Spurts of blood appeared on Alex's white pleated shirt. Sara watched transfixed as the two men grappled with each other, rolling along the railing of the yacht.

Viciously attacking again, Alex jammed his rival against the rail, delivering several hard fast jabs to his diaphragm as though Raphael were a punching bag, then jackknifed his knee into his groin. Raphael groaned in excruciating pain and sagged to the floor as if he suddenly turned to jelly. It all happened so blindingly fast that people stood awestruck by the explosion of fury. A woman screamed and pressed her fist to her mouth.

The sound jarred Sara from her frozen position. She rushed to her friend, a crumpled heap on the deck, and crouched beside him, realizing that even a man physically fit from playing tennis three times a week was no match for a man trained in the art of defense, honed by ten years' experience with the homicide and narcotics divisions. When her old friend unclenched his eyes, Alex's black temper surged at him in waves.

Alex stood over him, his legs still spread apart slightly in an aggressive stance. "You don't tell me who to stay away from." A jabbing finger accompanied his words.

Sara's choked protest followed on the heels of the fiery explosion. "Have you gone crazy? Look what you've done! Are you satisfied? Now will you leave him alone?"

The wind rushed around them. The blazing anger in Alex's eyes dimmed, and he finally showed signs of cooling down. The stunned spectators seemed agog for more. Alex adjusted his black tuxedo jacket, fixed the cuff links on his shirt with emphatic jerks of his hands and wrists, as though he were still letting off steam in fits and starts. The look in his eyes was abstracted but deadly. For a moment he turned to stare at Sara in the lengthening silence. His expression was enigmatic, as if he were reviewing something in his mind, like a man who had said or revealed more than he intended. Yet for a moment she got the impression he had forgotten she was there. Then it vanished.

Raphael was coming back to life. Propping himself against the side of the yacht, he staggered to his feet. Sara rose slowly with him, straightening. Having had the wind knocked out of him, he labored to get air back into his lungs. He held up his hands to keep her at bay, until he recovered. "I'm all right. Give me a few seconds to get my breath." When he straightened away from the side of the yacht he pulled himself together, then, leaning on Sara heavily, he propelled her toward the dance floor. "If we start dancing maybe people will stop looking at us." He pushed the words between clenched teeth with a wry smile.

By now they had attracted attention from most of the people on the starboard side of the yacht. Not wanting to remain the center of attention and to restore a sense of normalcy to the evening Sara went into

Raphael's arms. They danced knowing that all eyes were still focused intently on them. The Latin American band was still playing a romantic number, oblivious to or ignoring the violent skirmish that had taken place. Raphael leaned heavily on her, but slowly she felt him regaining his equilibrium.

Her pounding heart slowed down. Over her partner's shoulder, Sara shot a searing look of reproach at Alex, as if to say he had ruined the entire evening; she temporarily forgot it was Raphael who had made the first aggressive move. Completely unrepentant, Alex drilled his gaze into Sara for several long moments. Then he turned away, as if he had suddenly lost interest. She watched him rejoin a group of people, moving with that smooth indolent ease so familiar to her.

As they danced mechanically to the rhythmic pulsating music, Raphael gradually recovered. His dark eyes searched her face. "What was between you and him, Sara?" His voice was still a little airy, but he was almost back to normal. Pulling out a handkerchief she examined the gash where his cheekbone had slammed against the side of the yacht, then she dabbed at the cut solicitously.

"There's nothing between us now. It's over. It was over a long time ago. He just doesn't see it that way, that's all."

Smiling ruefully, he commented, "You will excuse me, Sara if I do not agree." His hand slid gingerly to his bruised diaphragm. Wincing again, he continued. "He acts like he thinks he owns you."

"Well, he doesn't. That's in his mind. It's not what I think."

Silently marveling at the assurance of her own
words, she continued to dart occasional glances at her
ex-husband, not entirely sure of what he might do
next. But after a while she tried to lose herself in the
music and the gaiety of the evening. She pressed her
face against the side of Raphael's, and they danced
with that slow rhythmic hip movement so characteristic of Latin American music.

"He's going to pay for this," he muttered in her ear.

Leaning back she looked at him. "It's over," she
said softly, looking into his eyes. "Try to forget it."

"This I cannot do, Sara."

Alarm shot through her. "Think it over," she
pleaded quietly. "When you cool down."

"*Si.* I will cool down and I will think it over. I
promise you."

As the evening progressed, the noisy party went into
high gear. The white spangled yacht cruised through
the Intracoastal Waterway, the palatial homes of Palm
Beach sliding by and waters churning and foaming in
the locks. Sara tried to forget the whole incident, tried
to forget that Alex was anywhere around. She tried to
forget the intensifying rivalry between the two men,
and the fact that she was now caught up in the cross
fire. Sometime later she saw Alex talking to some
dark-haired beauty with an avaricious gleam in her
eyes, whom she had seen with him earlier.

Late that night the yacht reached the last leg of the
return trip; it would be cruising into the marina soon.
The night closed around them like a velvet fist. Sara
and Raphael stood on deck chatting amiably to various people about inconsequential things. Conversations were winding down, and the music didn't sound

as effervescent as before. A few people who had consumed too much alcohol lurched around the deck laughing wildly and speaking incoherently.

When the yacht neared the tie-up, Sara caught a glimpse of Alex in a corner with the same dark-haired woman. The woman now had her arms linked around Alex's neck like a necklace, whispering in his ear, extending some kind of intimate invitation to him. His hands were resting on her waist, his head bent as if he were considering her invitation, but something in his stance held her away.

On top of everything Sara couldn't deny her feelings when she saw Alex with another woman. Something clenched; she thought it was her heart. Waiting impatiently at Raphael's side for the crew to tie up, she wanted only for the evening to come to an end. The long-anticipated glittering gala evening had turned into a full-blown disaster. She wanted only to put her feet on solid ground again and drive home.

Finally the crew was finished with the mooring and people left the opulent yacht in noisy bunches, drifting toward their parked cars scattered around the marina.

Raphael drove her home and walked her to her door. His face concealed by shadow, he kissed her and whispered in her ear. "Do not let anyone or anything poison your mind about me, Sara." He pulled back after saying good-night.

Standing in the doorway, she watched him slip into the Aston Martin and drive away. She felt very weary and confused by two persuasive human beings, each trying to convince her of something totally different. Whom was she to believe? Truth was always elusive, but especially when charged emotions were running high. The intense rivalry between Alex and Raphael couldn't be denied. She didn't care what Alex said about not letting personal emotions interfere with his professional judgment—she was sure now that it had. What was the truth? There was Alex and the way she still felt about him on one side, along with his suspicions and professional expertise; on the other side there was Raphael's background and charm, the close associations with her family and past and the way she felt about him, too. Bemused, she walked silently into the condo.

During the weeks that followed the cruise, Sara settled more into her work and her new way of life. The days rolled one into another; the newsroom had hit the doldrums with few big breaking stories and nothing terribly exciting happening. It was like that sometimes.

After her hectic life while chasing foreign assignments, she liked that things were peaceful and settled now. She enjoyed not having to live out of a suitcase anymore and congratulated herself on settling down to this easier, more civilized existence. All those years spent wandering had broadened her outlook, but they had also made her more appreciative of what was close at hand.

Yet Sara's new, more settled life was flawed by an underlying pervasive restlessness. There were signs and feelings she didn't want to give a name to that told her Alex had made deeper inroads into her mind and heart than she had thought. She often found herself driving a little too fast. Or spending a little more money than she should. And there were all those nights when she tossed and turned in her sleep, dreaming. Dreams of Alex, always Alex. The unrelenting restlessness told her something was missing from her life, that something always had been, that she was still looking for love. The constant pressure the restlessness exerted was dangerous, because it left her feeling vulnerable and exposed like some oversensitive nerve. She had the sensation that she was always burning, as if she had a sunburn that never faded. More times than she cared to count, Alex slid into her mind.

Occasionally she saw him in the course of her work. Once when she accompanied a reporter covering another drug bust, and again when Alex was giving evidence in court. Both times were from a comfortable distance. In such settings, with other people around him, he looked very authoritative, very professional and very street-smart. When their eyes met, they just regarded each other, and Sara gave him no encouragement, knowing he was too adept at stoking the banked passionate feelings that still existed between them. She had the sensation that he was waiting for the right moment to make his next move, that he still held some residual resentment over the past, that any minute all that fiery macho temperament would be released again. Nothing had really been resolved between them by the attempt to smooth things over. When he saw her, his eyes beamed the silent message: *We're not finished, you and me.*

She turned away, irritated. It didn't matter that she had explained to him how she felt; it made no difference to him at all.

* * *

When Sara walked into the photography department and then into the newsroom one Monday morning to check with her editor about her assignments, she sensed excitement in the air. There was the low hum of highly stimulated voices buzzing in unison, indicating a big story had broken. Intrigued and wondering what it was all about, she headed over to a group of people to find out.

The city editor was talking to two of his best reporters—Herb Olsen and Jack Paterson. Leaning against the doorframe, Sara inquired, "What's going on?"

"I'm glad you're here, Sara," the editor said. "There's something big going on at the Miami Police Department. Remember that last big seizure of cocaine and money we covered?"

"You mean the five-million-dollar shipment intercepted at the ranch near Punta Gorda?"

"Yes. And rumors are flying fast and thick that part of it is missing from the police holding warehouse. They suspect some of the men in the department helped themselves. The whole thing is blowing up in their face and all they can do is ride out the storm. I want you and Herb to get over to the department and see what you can get. The men in Centac who made the bust are the ones under suspicion, because someone traded information for some kind of immunity and pointed the finger at them. The guy in charge of that special unit—what's his name?" The editor snapped his fingers as he drew a mental blank.

"Cordera. Alex Cordera," Sara inserted quietly.

"Get some really good stills of this guy, Sara. I want to see the emotional strain, the tension in the face of a man with his career and his integrity on the line. This isn't the first time the department has been faced with corruption charges. The public remembers that, and they'll want to read about it, see results, see some heads roll. There's nothing worse than a bad cop."

Sara nodded, feeling all the blood drain from her face. He was talking about Alex. She maintained an outward calm and made no comments. A few moments later, after collecting her gear, she accompanied Herb Olsen and two reporters going out on another assignment to the elevators.

"When something like this happens in the police department there's wall-to-wall paranoia," Herb observed as they all stepped inside the elevator. "Everybody suspects everyone else of being in on it. Cordera may be the man implicated, but I know from past experience that emotions will be running high everywhere you look."

The other two reporters stood talking in low speculative tones, but Sara was noncommittal. Emotions were running high inside her, too, very telling emotions; she was practically vibrating with them.

Alex's words came back to her again with reverberating force: *There's still plenty going on between you and me.* Love cut deep. Nothing else told her more unequivocally or with more impact that she was still half in love with him. All these years had rolled by and somehow she had kept him locked away in her heart, deceived herself by telling herself she had forgotten him. But she had never forgotten him or stopped loving him. She had never stopped caring. Nothing showed her that more clearly than what was happening now. She cared about Alex Cordera, she cared about what happened to him—she cared very much. She had no wish to see him publicly humiliated, to see all that he had worked so hard for in jeopardy. This suspicion and the harsh glare of publicity could destroy a career overnight. When mud was thrown, a little always stuck, even to those cleared of suspicion.

As the doors to the elevator slid open, she heard the last snatch of conversation between the two reporters. "We've got our work cut out for us. You know what it's like with cops—they close ranks when any one of them gets into trouble, even when they suspect each other."

The Miami Police Department looked as though it were under siege. Uniformed police officers hung around outside the building, trying to keep some kind of order as newspaper reporters got out of cars and TV crews emerged from minivans. Obviously word had leaked out everywhere.

Once inside Sara was caught up in the melee of jabbing elbows, pointed cameras and shouted questions, which the commander of the Narcotics Division fobbed off with terse replies.

"Two boards of inquiry are being set up. Internal Affairs is conducting their own investigation on the department's behalf. But the Drug Enforcement Agency, which was also involved in this major cocaine seizure, wants to conduct theirs separately."

Herb Olsen fired a shrewd question at him. "Is the DEA setting up its own board of inquiry because they worked with Centac or because they don't trust anyone in the department who has been exposed to temptation for any length of time—including the people who work in Internal Affairs?'' Members of the media around them roared with laughter.

The commander didn't see the funny side of it. ''Any more remarks like that and you won't get any more comments from me.''

''Who are the officers implicated?''

The commander confirmed that it was the members of Centac and told them their names. He answered questions on how much cocaine was missing, then held up his hands saying that was all he could tell them for the time being. It was clear to Sara and the other journalists that defensive feelings were running high in the department.

She gazed around restlessly, searching for Alex, and finally located him. He was being mobbed, but he wasn't answering questions nor was he running or hiding. In that familiar impatient stance, hands propped on hips, head angled slightly to one side, he was talking to some official in the corridor near the water fountain. She called out his name, trying to attract his attention above the hubbub so she could get some good stills while others tried to get a statement from him. As usual he had an uncanny perception of her presence. The dark head and broad-shouldered back swung around, his gaze turning unerringly in her direction. There was a chilling look in his eyes when he saw her.

The click of her camera and the repeated ignition of the flash reassured her that she was focused on her job, getting the tense, beleaguered expression the editor wanted. But Alex's icy regard left her feeling shaky. If the fine reputation of Centac wasn't sufficiently intact when all the dust settled, the unit might be disbanded—a sobering thought for the man who had built it up to what it was, who had been responsible for its impressive record of convictions.

Ever since she ran into Alex that first night at the Polo Lounge, she had often longed for someone or something to knock him down a peg or two. But now that her wish seemed on the verge of coming true, she knew she never had wanted it to happen. To see this proud man with a lust for life brought to his knees in any respect was something that she had no desire to see at all.

Chapter 5

In the days that followed events moved so quickly that they blurred one into another. Sara heard that Alex had been relieved of the command of his unit until both boards of inquiry had completed their independent investigations and were satisfied with their findings. Half a dozen times she had telephoned him and half a dozen times he refused her calls.

Putting down the phone again after what she promised herself was the last time she would attempt to reach him, Sara sank back in her desk chair. She desperately wanted to tell him that she was on his side, but she couldn't even get near him. It was as if the proud Latin side of his nature had erected an impassable barrier between them. His refusal to take her calls told her only one thing—he wanted nothing from her. This cold shoulder, this professional aloofness was something new to her. She much preferred the short-fused side of his nature to this.

Later that day she heard via the newsroom that Alex had opted to return to homicide, where he had started out, until the investigation was completed. The headlines in the first edition of the *Miami Guardian* the next morning were ugly: FBI Probes Miami PD Narcotics Unit, Cordera Denies Corruption Allegations.

The *Guardian* pursued the developments of the story. More and more pictures were required to fan and hold the interest of the public. Sara had the unenviable task of getting some of the pictures. On two consecutive days she spent hours hanging around the police department while the separate boards of inquiry convened. After being grilled by their superiors, Alex and his men had to run the media gauntlet.

That afternoon, when the doors finally opened, she and the other journalists swarmed around the men emerging from some inner sanctum. Grim-faced but dignified, Alex looked neither right nor left as he charged through the mob.

Sara knew she had to attract his attention to shoot the angles of his face she wanted. "Lieutenant Cordera, this way please."

The sound of her voice made his dark head turn her way. The explosive look in his eyes immediately warned her that he was getting really upset at seeing Sara in her professional capacity. He didn't lessen the ground-eating strides as he continued on his way, so she had to keep moving to keep up with him. He wasn't doing her any favors. Sensitive to many expressions of his face, she was working fast to get plenty of shots for the editor to choose from, hoping for that one perfect photo.

His gaze swung to hers contemptuously. "You keep bustin' my ass, Sara. What do you want from me? Maybe you want some *exclusive* coverage. Come up and see me tonight. I'll give you all the exclusive coverage you can handle."

Fellow police officers around him, as well as most of the reporters, laughed when he fired the words at her with plenty of innuendo in his tone; no doubt remained in anybody's mind as to what he meant.

She lowered her camera to look at him. "I'm not laughing, Lieutenant Cordera."

"Neither am I, Sara." Pushing through a set of fire doors so hard they threatened to shake loose from their hinges, he continued on his way out of the building without missing a beat.

She knew she could get more shots of him on his way to his car, but her heart wasn't in it. His sharp rebuke, his jeering words, stayed with her as she walked to her own car. The pressure he was under, the memories of what they had once been to each other, the feelings that still lingered inside them both, all reverberated inside her heart and mind long after he had driven away. Her hands shook as she lowered the camera into the camera bag. A man under so much fire was bound to lash out. But his contemptuous look had accused her of picking over his carcass like the rest of the vultures from the media. It was a look that told her in spite of everything that had happened between them he expected more, a lot more, from her. No matter how much she rationalized that she had a job to do, that she couldn't let her personal feelings get in the way, it didn't make her feel any better. Instead she felt punctured by his humiliating gibes. He had scored some direct hits. When Alex was angry, especially with a woman, he was deadly.

Sara had just finished showering, her hair still wrapped in a white turban, when the doorbell rang. She tore off the turban and flung it aside. She tightened the belt of her long white terry robe around her waist and rushed to answer it. The robe flapped around her bare legs as she padded across the thick carpet in bare feet.

Shock rattled through her like a dry wind when she opened the door. Alex hung in the doorway, grinning down at her, hands propped on either side of the doorframe.

"What's the matter, surprised to see me? This is your big chance, Sara, to cash in our former *friendship*. You can shoot all the film you want now. I'm here. Where's your sister?"

"Out for the evening."

"That's good, because I wanted to talk to you alone."

"Listen—I'm sorry if it looks that way, but I'm not trying to cash in on anything."

She backed away when he stepped inside uninvited, closing the door behind him with an unreadable expression in his eyes. When he was like this she never knew what was coming next. Before he could say anything else, she rushed on.

"I wanted to tell you that I don't enjoy hounding you with the rest of the media. I don't believe the corruption charges. But you didn't give me a chance to tell you that." She stepped back again, trying to hang on to her composure.

Alex's lazy gaze slid over her appreciatively. "That's what I like about you. I can always count on you, Sara." He continued to smile at her but his words dripped with irony.

"Why are you here?"

"Remember the last time we saw each other?"

"The night of the cruise?"

"I want you to think about that night, Sara."

"I'd rather not." She swung away, intending to go sit down, but his next words stopped her short.

"Remember how Raphael became aggressive?"

She swung sharply back to face him. "I remember you looking as though you wanted to kill him, if that's what you mean," she accused softly.

"I want to know what you told Raphael that night."

"Told him? Told him about what? I had nothing to tell him." She shrugged, holding up her hands in confusion. Alex was like a compelling movie star on a giant screen—it was difficult to take her eyes off him for any length of time. But when she looked straight at him she found it difficult to think straight.

He moved close to her. He reached out a hand to capture the curve of her neck, then slid it slowly inside the collar of her robe. He gauged her reaction to him. They gazed steadily at each other.

"You still like my hands on you? Nothing changes that, does it?" he announced with a knowing expression.

Closing her eyes at the sensation of his hand sliding downward, inching its way from her bare warm shoulder and hovering just above the swell of her breast, she breathed a husky protest and repeated the question more forcefully. "Told him what?"

"I never could keep my hands off you, could I?" His eyes darkened when she opened hers. His tone became an intimate caress, yet remained full of menace. "What did you tell Cruzero?"

"About what?" she demanded with a mixture of agitation and genuine puzzlement. "What are you driving at?"

"Think back, Sara. Who started the trouble that night?"

She frowned trying to remember. "He shoved you first. He said something like, 'She is with me, you stay away,' and he pushed you, I think. It all happened so fast, I can't...remember exactly."

"Did you ever wonder why he got aggressive?"

"It was obvious. Because he thought you were trying to move in on his date."

"Think harder," he said, his voice developing a compelling rough edge. "Did anything else happen that night that would make him aggressive? What did you talk about?" When she frowned again, he added, "I warned you about him when you came to my office. I showed you a file. That was in confidence between you and me. Did you tell him about that?"

Now she realized what he was driving at. Her body tensed as she remembered. Recognition dawned slowly, along with the memory of the halfhearted conversation she had initiated with Raphael that night about his business associations.

"We did talk a little that night about his business associations. After what you told me I was worried about him. I wondered if he appreciated the risks he was taking even if his associations were indirect ones. I told him that a confidential source informed someone in the newsroom—"

Alex grabbed both her shoulders and shook her. "Informed someone of what—that there was a folder on *my* desk in the Narcotics Division?"

Words rattled out of her mouth. "I said a confidential source—"

"A confidential source told someone in the newsroom?" He closed his eyes, obviously savoring the naiveté of her remark. "You little fool. Do you know how long it took him to figure out who your confidential source was, Sara? Maybe two minutes tops. Did you ever stop to think what the consequences would be when he figured it out?"

Dismay pooled in the depths of her eyes. She stared at him, stunned. No, she hadn't stopped to think. Her inexperience and her conviction that her old friend was innocent contributed to her lack of consideration of what the aftereffects would be.

The look in Alex's eyes confirmed her dismay; the force of his words underlined his conviction. "From your remarks, all he had to do was put two and two together, Sara, to know that he's under investigation. Do you think you fooled him that night in the Polo Lounge about our former relationship? He wants me off his back and out of the way. And he wants you. I was set up, Sara. Can you think of anyone who has more reason to set me up? That's why I'm facing corruption charges. Now we *both* know who's behind them."

"How can you be so sure?" she lashed out with tears stinging the backs of her eyes. "You're always so sure of everything, aren't you?'' Her tone was low, tremulous and accusing, but she was shaking inside with emotion, her mind reeling from the effect of his words. She held up her hand in a slicing gesture that said she had had enough.

''I never asked to get in the middle of all this. I wish I had never come back to Miami. I never wanted this.'' The choked words tumbled from her lips. Once again, her inexperience was causing him trouble.

Remorse shone in her eyes. Something inside Alex eased off and he caught her again, pulling her close to him.

''No, Sara. You never asked, honey. But you are.'' His tone changed from threatening to a low intimate caress. Sharp-edged humor lit his burnt sienna eyes, making them lazy with speculation. ''You know there's only one way to get out of the middle. You want to know what it is?''

She relaxed against him, suddenly weary. The emotional strain of seeing Alex under fire, and now the harsh words dealt out to her, had taken their toll, knocked the stuffing out of her. She was like putty in his hands. It never occurred to her that was exactly how he intended her to feel, that he was an expert at breaking people down, getting them to do what he wanted. She stood acquiescently in his arms, forgetting for a moment any thoughts of resistance. Her hands rested on his shoulders near his neck.

''What is it?'' she murmured, her eyes searching his.

''Come over to my side, Sara. That's how you get out of the middle. That's where you belong.'' He trailed the words against the side of her face while he

pulled her closer. The warmth of her body met his.
Her whole body came alive under his touch. His hands
slid down over the terry robe, kneading her flesh,
molding her into the hard vitality of his. She wanted
to help him, not hurt him—the thought eddied inside
her.

"You're either with me or against me. There's no
other way."

"I am on your side. If you had taken my calls you
would have known that from the very beginning." She
leaned back in his arms so that he could see for himself the sincerity behind her words.

His eyes measured her response. "Prove it, Sara."

"How?"

"You know what I want. I want to start seeing you
again. This is driving us both crazy—being in the same
town, running into each other, over and over. The
tension keeps building. We can't go on tormenting
each other like this. I *have* to see you again."

She was so surprised by his admission of need she
didn't say anything. But he didn't press her for an answer right away. Slowly releasing her, he stepped back
with a look that said he was reluctant to go. He
checked his wristwatch.

"I have to go now. I'm working. I've already taken
more time out than I should. I want you to think
about that tonight. Okay?"

"Okay," she murmured.

"I'm going to find you tomorrow and I want an
answer by then. Where will you be tomorrow?"

"On the beach near my condo. I'll be going for a
swim first thing in the morning."

* * *

The next morning was a beautiful balmy Sunday.
The drive to the beach took Alex only about fifteen
minutes. The dazzling sunshine bathed everything in
brilliant light. The vast stretches of silver beach, the
turquoise sky and the stands of palmetto palms clustered near the shore, their saw-toothed fronds sway-
ing lazily in the breeze, were a familiar and welcome
sight. His mind was on other things, however, not the
beauty of his surroundings.

When Alex stepped out of his car he combed the
beach for Sara. From the ridged sand dune he picked
her out. Tanned and curvaceous in a flowered bikini
that showed off her spectacular figure to perfection,
Sara looked like a sea nymph emerging from the water, her slicked-back hair accentuating her cheekbones.

Seven years ago, before they'd married, they had
often come to this deserted stretch of beach, Alex remembered. More than once they had been forced to
get up and leave abruptly because the fires between
them burned too hot, and he came close to making
love to her on the spot. The beach was a secluded one,
but there was always the possibility of an interloper,
the unexpected intrusion of a solitary beachcomber.

She hadn't seen him yet; he stood several hundred
yards away. He lit a cigarette as he gathered his
thoughts. The night before he had softened Sara up
with the knowledge that Raphael was behind the corruption charges. He had no proof, but there was no
doubt in his mind. What he hadn't told her was that
the investigators had already cracked the informant
who had leveled the charges against Centac; Alex

knew that he and his men were already in the clear. In exchange for getting his younger brother out of prison on parole, the informant had confessed that he had been put up to it. Fearful of harsh reprisals, however, he wouldn't name names, neither of the man who had hired him to make the false accusation nor of the men who actually did steal the cocaine. Alex had promised the informant that his confession would be covered up, made to look as though Internal Affairs had doubted his testimony.

He had neglected to tell Sara any of this because he wanted to capitalize on the advantage of her ignorance. He had used this advantage and gotten the results he wanted last night. The flare of guilt in her eyes, the look of remorse over her naive blunder had told him all he needed to know. He had struck a raw nerve; her inexperience had worked for him this time instead of against him. Now he meant to move in for the kill. He had given her plenty of time to think. If his instincts were right, if she wanted him as much as he wanted her, the rest of his plan would fall into place. But Sara could always spring surprises—he had learned that the hard way seven years ago—so he wasn't counting on her reaction; he was only following his instincts about what he thought she would do. If he was right, his plan was moving ahead and moving ahead fast. He wanted her back in his life and in his bed and he wanted to see the look on Raphael's face when he succeeded. When Raphael heard the news Alex wanted him to lose his head, to slip up, to start making the mistakes that were going to cost him his freedom, the ones he hadn't made up to now. Love could make a fool out of anyone; no one knew that

better than Alex did. This woman had already fooled
him once. He wasn't going to give her the chance to do
it again.

He dropped the cigarette, crushing it into the sand,
and strode down the beach to let Sara know he was
there. The words *I have to see you again* came back to
him. A nagging voice inside his head said that it was
no lie.

As Sara moved from the water to the shore, Alex's
words about "getting out of the middle" came once
again into her mind. He wanted her back. It was there
in his eyes and in his entire manner. She wanted to
answer that desire. Everything inside her responded to
it. Alex had robbed her of her peace of mind ever since
she came back to Miami.

The soft waves lapped around her ankles as she
walked out of the gentle surf. With both hands she
reached up to slick the wet hair away from her face,
tightly closing her eyes to squeeze saltwater out of her
thick lashes. When she opened them she focused hazily on the ridge above the shoreline and saw a man
approaching.

Mirrored sunglasses could not disguise the face of
the man she had known intimately. She knew Alex had
won this silent battle of the wills. Or was it desire that
had won? She could no longer think objectively; she
only knew she wanted to be with him. A black polo-
style shirt spanned the breadth of his shoulders and
flatly muscled torso, casual pants outlined the long
hard legs as he walked slowly toward her. Standing
before her, he pulled off the sunglasses and stuck them
into his pocket.

''Well, did you think about what I said?''

''A good part of the night,'' she said, laughing softly.

They were two people surrounded by a tropical paradise that could have been frozen in time on a picture postcard. But there wasn't anything frivolous about the look they exchanged. The good-natured attitude he adopted didn't disguise that he was a man very intent on getting what he wanted.

''Are you with me or against me, Sara?'' His hands closed on her bare shoulders, burning like the sun on her skin.

She leaned in to him as he drew her inside the circle of his arms. ''I want to be with you,'' she whispered. ''Let's start seeing each other again.''

''Let's start now.''

His eyes gleamed with warm possessiveness. Turning on the charm, he'd murmured the words against the side of her neck and pulled her toward his heated body. Her hands rested on the impressive strength of his flexed arms. Weakness attacked first her mind and then her legs.

''I have to see you again, Sara. Don't keep me hanging around.''

When he put it that way, everything seemed so simple. The husky pitch of his tone, the heartfelt need, tore away at her last shred of resistance. When he was like this, she could refuse him nothing. ''Yes, now, this minute.'' She laughed. For several dizzying moments her mind went blank. Only the hungry demanding kisses covering her face, her neck and finally her lips made any impression as his lean hard strength enveloped her.

* * *

A kind of courtship began. Alex's previous anger evaporated. It was like the sun coming out. He became affectionate, tender, attentive, even playful. Sara felt bowled over. She marveled as he seemed to undergo a personality change.

But it was not just seeing her again that brought about the change in Alex. It was also because the charges against him and Centac had been dropped. When she heard the news at work a few days after she had met him on the beach she had been filled with a sense of euphoria. When Alex had confirmed it at dinner that night it felt like Christmas.

Now when he regarded her with one of those lazy looks of possessiveness, Alex was if anything even more devastating than before. After taking her out again during the week, he announced that he wanted her to come to dinner at his family's home on Sunday.

Sunday afternoon they drove along one of the five causeways linking Miami with Miami Beach. Alex sat behind the wheel, looking relaxed. Sara was not feeling so relaxed. The Sunday family gathering was a weekly ritual for the Corderas. Like most Cubans they were very family oriented and conservative in their politics and outlook. She had been to several Sunday gatherings when Alex and she were a couple seven years ago. How would his family react to seeing her with him again? What did they think about the woman who had run out on him?

"You told them you were bringing me?" Sara queried with a sidelong glance.

He kept his attention on the road, then turned back to her. "I thought we would surprise them."

"Surprise them? Alex, I don't want to surprise them!" Her outburst was spontaneous, and when she saw the lines around his mouth deepen she felt like an idiot.

Amusement flowed into his words; he was enjoying himself immensely. "Sara, do you think I would walk in there with you after seven years and not say a word? I told them we were seeing each other again."

Irritated because he had gotten the best of her, she turned away, adding in a low voice, "I'm never sure what you will or won't do."

"That is an accusation I could level at you," he fired back low and quick. Sara got the message, it was another reference to the past.

Her gaze followed the shining waters surrounding the causeways. Ever since she had agreed to see him again, she knew deep inside that in spite of Alex's outwardly passionate nature, the attention he showered on her, all the smooth Cuban charm, there was a part of himself he still kept in reserve. It was almost as if a part of him didn't want her to love him. Perhaps more than his ego had been wounded when she left him. All she knew was that she was being tested somehow. She wasn't sure what the outcome would be. Her thoughts leaped back to seven years ago when she was so sure he'd thank her someday for letting him off the hook. She couldn't have been more wrong about that.

He shot her a sidelong look, obviously noticing the apprehension in her eyes. The lines around his mouth

deepened again. "Stay cool, Sara. You have nothing
to worry about, not from my family."

His last words did little to reassure her. He made it
sound as though she had something to worry about
from *him*. Her imagination was working overtime, she
thought. She was definitely on edge, understandably
so.

When they reached his house, the car cruised to a
stop and Alex turned to her. Sensing her continuing
unease, Alex told her warmly that it was his parents'
wedding anniversary and that no one was going to do
or say anything that would spoil the occasion. They
walked up to the house, his arm around her waist.

Alex's mother greeted them at the door. Sara leaned
down to kiss her on the cheek. The diminutive dark-
haired woman regarded her warmly, hugging her affectionately. "Sara, it's so good to see you again. Are
you happy to be back in Miami?"

"Yes, very."

"Everybody is out on the patio," Alex's mother
announced as they moved in that direction.

They walked toward the back of the house, then out
onto a large flower-choked patio. Suddenly they were
the cynosure of all eyes. Alex's sisters and brothers sat
in deck chairs, their children playing in the pool or
near their parents, toys scattered everywhere. Only his
immediate family knew what Sara and Alex had once
been to each other, making her return with Alex especially poignant and romantic like something in a
tormented Latin American love song. Alex's hand
tightened at her waist, and he murmured something
reassuring in her ear. It was moments like these when
Sara knew why it was so easy to lose her head over

him, to fall head over heels in love with him again. What woman could resist the protective, possessive attentiveness of the compelling man at her side? Nothing could quench the momentum of desire set in motion between them now. Their presence first silenced, then stimulated everyone into animated conversation. Suddenly everyone seemed to want to talk at once. The conversation flowed easily back and forth with rapid staccato energy. The warm silent message in Alex's eyes told her everything was going to be okay, to relax and enjoy the afternoon.

"Sara, Alex tells us you are now a photographer with the *Miami Guardian,*" his mother said. "And before this you traveled around the world working in many countries."

She drifted with his mother and one sister toward some chairs on the patio, talking about the difficulties of a photographer getting in and out of Cuba. His other sister and brothers were watching the children, who occasionally stopped playing to look at Sara and smile shyly. When she glanced back over her shoulder she could see Alex had gone to talk with his father and new brother-in-law.

The conversation was lively as they caught up on events in the family, and the comings and goings of people they knew. Alex's mother introduced the children to Sara one by one—some of them babies when she had last seen them, some of them not yet born. The easy conversation continued nonstop. For Sara the entire day had a dreamlike quality to it, like one of those overblown opulent films shot through a diffused lens. She found the visit much easier than she'd expected, glad to fit back in. It was almost as if sev-

eral pages from the past had been pulled out, then torn
up and thrown away on the afternoon breeze.

Alex sprawled his powerful frame in the chair beside her, resting an arm across the back of her chair.
The gleam of possession in his eyes spoke for itself.
Nothing she could do or say could offset the drugging
effect of it or of his nearness. But even when he was
completely at ease, Sara noticed, the charged side of
his personality was never far from the surface, especially when his newly married sister and brother-in-law
appeared. Whenever his new brother-in-law spoke or
addressed him, a steely aspect developed in Alex's
eyes. His sister Lourdis sat on her other side. They had
been talking for several minutes about places they had
both traveled to when Lourdis's expression grew serious.

"How do you find Alex? Do you think he has
changed much?"

Sara shook her head with a smile. He was more or
less just as she remembered him, a little older looking, a little more toughened by his work, maybe.

"Alex has been working too hard. You should be
warned. We see a change in him since he became head
of Centac. At first we thought he was a man with a
mission. Now his mission has become an obsession."

While he was talking to his brother on his right, Alex's sharp ears picked up his name on his sister's lips.
He turned sharply to query Sara. "What is she telling
you about me?" Then he addressed his sister with a
deceptive smile creeping across his face. "Lourdis,
what are you filling Sara's head with?"

"I was just telling her that you are too self-
disciplined when it comes to your work, that it is

reaching the point of near obsession. I'm doing her a favor and warning her about how you have changed.''

He swung his powerful body around to confront them both. ''Doing her a favor, warning her? Is that what you call it?'' Leaning forward in the chair he jabbed a playful finger in the direction of his sister's nose. ''Remember what I said, Lourdis. Keep that beautiful nose out of my business and nothing I do or say will offend you.'' He surveyed his sister with some sharp-edged humor in his eyes. ''Don't do her any more favors. Okay?''

With her head held high Lourdis turned away to resume a conversation with her younger sister on the other side of the table, completely ignoring Alex.

Alex faced Sara, resting his forearms on his spread knees. He shot her a rueful glance. The expression told her he and Lourdis didn't see eye to eye on something else. It was her new husband, Leo. Alex lowered his voice, so Leo, who was talking to Alex's father on the other side of the patio, couldn't hear.

''She doesn't like it when I remind her of some of Leo's courtroom antics. Or what he refers to as the 'creative practice of criminal law.' Or the fact that he makes big money defending drug traffickers. Leo sees it as his goal to provide the best possible defense, to win any way he can within the law. My brother-in-law used to be the prosecutor for the state attorney's office until he switched sides. He's got a reputation for using every trick in the book and is limited only by his imagination. When I remind her of these things she tells me I'm becoming obsessed with my job. Those early days, watching our parents work so hard when they first came over from Cuba has left us all fiercely driven. I want to put away people like Cruzero. My sister wants to climb the social ladder. But she's wrong about me.''

Catching hold of her arm with the air of a man who didn't want to lose something he had only recently gained back, he said, ''Like most Cubans I have the northern work ethic, but I have the southern joy of life. I'm not obsessed with my job. Don't let anything anyone says get to you, Sara. Make up your own mind about me.''

For a moment Raphael's words came back to her. They had used almost the exact same words to defend themselves, she realized.

''I never really did get to know you. Did I?'' Was she falling in love again with a man she didn't really know? Was that possible?

His eyes locked with hers. ''*We* never really got to know each other, Sara.''

Resting an arm across the back of her chair, he angled his head to the side of her face, teasing her with the soft rhythmic roll of his words. ''You have a second chance. Don't blow it this time and and maybe you will get to know me. If you're lucky,'' he teased, biting her earlobe.

At exactly that moment his mother's voice floated over from the other side of the patio. ''Alejandro?''

Alex turned his head in her direction as he said to Sara, ''When she calls me that she means business.''

Amused and bemused by his words, she watched him go. By the time Alex returned, all the food and wine had been set out on the table. Everyone drew their chairs closer around the table while Alex's father rose to his feet to say a few well-chosen words about being married for forty years to the same woman and to reminisce about the very hard years when the family first came to the States. They had come from Cuba during the first wave of immigration in the sixties, forced to leave everything behind but the clothes on their backs.

Alex's fingers walked across Sara's bare back, catching the tab of the zipper at the back of her white halter dress. With a silent erotic teasing message he began pulling it up and down, while his father continued reminiscing about how hard it was starting over from scratch. Sara inched forward inconspicuously to get away from Alex's taunting fingers. But his hand curved around her bare shoulder and rested there, her skin burning underneath his fingers. Sara listened as his father concluded his remarks with words of wisdom spoken with quiet dignity.

"I have learned a few things in forty years of marriage." He angled his head toward his wife, then continued. "The love between a man and a woman is a beautiful thing. It is a fortress against the harshness of life and all kinds of adversity." He lifted a realistic eyebrow. "But it can also be the most destructive relationship on earth." He seemed to be looking in Sara's and Alex's direction. Glasses were raised all around the table, their pale golden contents glittering in the sunlight as they clinked delicately in the toast.

Sipping the wine, Sara looked around pensively over the rim of the glass. A warm flush spread across her skin; it was as if the words just spoken were designed for her and Alex. Their subtle warning made a chill go down her spine. Alex was somehow both enigmatic and forceful in his silence alongside her. She felt relieved when the moment had gone and food was passed down the table.

"Are you sorry you spent so much time away?" Lourdis asked Sara.

"No. Now I appreciate things here more. That's what spending any length of time in a foreign country does for you," she added, laughing softly.

"She means me," Alex interceded on his own behalf.

"My brother is very modest." Lourdis remarked with a smile that said her brother was back in her good graces for the time being.

When they arrived on Sara's doorstep it was dark. Alex lost no time and started to kiss her. Her hand rested on the back of his neck. His burning gaze dropped to the shadowy cleft of her breasts where his hand invaded the halter neckline of her dress. The darkening aspect of his eyes excited her as she excited him. She wanted his hands on her. Suddenly his kisses were everywhere—rhythmic, ardent, tender, covering her face and neck. She turned her face into his neck, pressing her lips against the cords there as he caressed the other side of her face with heated kisses.

"This is all happening too fast again," she murmured breathlessly, trying to grasp at something to slow the descent down the slippery slope of passion.

"It can't be too soon for me." Alex was pushing her over the edge with a distinct purpose in mind. He wanted her back. Sara wasn't entirely sure of what conditions he was laying down. There was still a hard-edged enigmatic quality to him behind all this red-hot desire.

While she still had some reason left, she bargained. "Alex." She caught his hand, attempting to restrain him for a moment. "What's it going to cost us both?"

"It's not going to cost us anything because it's what we both want," he assured her. With his eyes narrowed by desire, his tone low-pitched and husky, he was obviously reluctant to concede anything else to her, or to give her the chance to lay down any specific conditions. "Whatever you want, Sara, you got it. Open the door and let me in."

Turning her gently around, he guided her hand as she put the key in the lock. He pressed himself intimately against her back so that she could feel his unmistakable arousal. The sheer maleness of him coupled with *her* already aroused state made her hand shake slightly as she twisted the key in the lock. Covering her hand with his, he steadied it, biting her neck, sending sensations streaming down her bare shoulder. She shivered in reaction.

He breathed the words, *I want you.* Propelling her across the threshold he shoved the door closed behind them and took her handbag out of her hands, tossing it impatiently out of the way onto the nearest chair. He pulled her back into his arms; their kisses grew hungrier and rougher. Unable to get enough of each other, unable to make up for the seven years that had gone by, they had no desire to talk. They only wanted to quench the surging passion between them.

Pressing her against the wall, locking his eyes with hers, he maneuvered the zipper down on her dress, then pulled the dress from her shoulders, his mouth capturing hers at the same time. A sense of urgency consumed him. They couldn't wait. It had been too

long. Foreplay was not required or wanted. They had
been engaged in a kind of extended foreplay ever since
they first saw each other again in the Polo Lounge. His
lips were mobile, moving from her neck to her cheek
back to her mouth. Her hands locked on his hard
waist; she wanted him closer while his hands worked
the dress down over her hips, then searched for the
hook on her bra. Desire crawled down her legs and
arms, bringing a gnawing ache that bloomed deep between her thighs. The tremors of surrender and reawakened passion racked her body. Satisfaction shone
in his eyes. She was hot for him and he knew it. All
pretense at control disappeared.

They lurched toward the bedroom as if driven by
blind instinct. Kissing her deeply now, molding her
trembling body into his, Alex brought her into a fevered haze of arousal. His hands worked feverishly at
his belt, then he pulled off his pants and yanked his
shirt over his head. Entirely naked, he rocked her
against his thighs with his hand at the base of her spine
urging her into him, pushing himself against her in a
rhythmic assault, groaning his pleasure against her lips
before he deepened the kiss again. Incoherent words
of passion tumbled from his lips before he deepened
the kiss again. The raw passion carried them toward
the bed. Rolling her onto her back on the soft mat-
tress, his hard body finally covered hers.

Chapter 6

When Sara sleepily rolled over in bed the next morning, her arm struck something hard as granite. Her eyelids fluttered open. She turned her head slowly to one side. Through a thick screen of eyelashes she focused hazily on a deeply bronzed jutting shoulder blade. Sweeping upward, her eyes scaled the intimidating brawny shoulders of a sleeping man, whose dark head was buried in the pillow a few inches from her own.

The mist of sleep began to lift. The night before came back to her in brilliant rippling flashes, the erotic colors of desire surging through her again. She shuddered imperceptibly. A warm flush of pleasure spread across her skin. Time had not diminished their hunger for each other; abstinence had only intensified their strong needs. The twisted tangle of sheets indicated to the turbulence of their attempt to make up for

lost time. Alex's whispered exhortations in the dead of
the night came floating back into her mind now. She
remembered him above her, his eyes heavy with desire, his forearms braced on either side of her face,
looking down at her. She thought she remembered him
saying, "Sara, *mi querida perdida.*" Then, he hadn't
been interested in talking. Neither had she. The silent
language of their need for each other said it all.

The harsh light of morning always cast a sobering
perspective on things, especially emotions. Sometimes it was as if there were two sets of emotions people lived by inside one body, those that ruled the day
and those that ruled the night. The crazy things people did in the dark had no connection with the sober
demands of the harsh glare of daylight.

Was she in over her head again? She couldn't say;
she couldn't think straight enough to be objective. She
propped herself up on one arm to focus hazily on the
bedside clock. It was Monday. In a few moments the
clock radio would go off. She slumped back against
the pillow. There was a low groan from the sleeping
man beside her. An arm snaked out, locking around
her neck and dragging her beside him.

"Come here." The muffled voice sounded like a vibrating drain. Warm lips explored her neck, kindling
a reawakening sensation. In moments they were kissing and Alex had her pinned beneath him, covering
her with his hard body. In between kisses she murmured that it was Monday. He lifted his head, sleep-
narrowed eyes checking the steel Rolex on his wrist.

"We have to get up," she reminded him, studying
the face above hers.

He didn't agree. Having decided there was still time, he surveyed her with a warm look in his burnt sienna eyes.

"How is the lady of my life this morning?" Volumes of meaning flowed into his words but none more so than the long look of assessing male satisfaction mirrored in his eyes.

In her heart she was already committed to him, but she was not ready to say it out loud. Her own recklessness made her reluctant to take the final step to tell him how much she loved him or that she wanted to spend her life with him.

"Did you hear what I said?" He tapped her nose with a demanding playfulness. "I want a little feedback here. Are you always this quiet after a guy makes mad, passionate love to you half the night?"

"I'm crazy about you. You know that," she murmured. "Dangerously so."

"Why do you say that?" The enigmatic wariness crept into his expression, the same expression that she could never pin down.

"I'm not sure," she said, looking deep into his eyes. They gazed at each other for a long moment. Then her mind took a practical turn. "You should dress and leave here before my sister gets up, and before the neighbors see your car parked outside. There's an old busybody next door who keeps track of the comings and goings of everyone who lives on this street. I don't want to provide her with grist for her mill, something to tell the whole neighborhood." She breathed the words against his ear as he lowered his head to nuzzle her neck. "Alex, please be good." There was a soft pleading tone to her voice, asking him to behave.

Shooting her a look that said he enjoyed the potential embarrassment his presence might cause, he lifted a playful eyebrow.

"So you don't want your sister or anyone in the neighborhood to know what goes on between you and me? They only have to see the way I look at you and they will know." He spoke softly, his teasing macho grin tormenting her.

"Maybe not," she conceded, while his hands were locking on the curve of her hips with a distinct purpose in mind. The prospect of getting him to move seemed to be fast eluding her.

"Don't you have to go to work? Isn't it Monday?"

Sliding down in the bed, he buried his face between her breasts. "You are right, it is Monday. But you are trying to get rid of me," he taunted. "I don't like it when a woman tries to get rid of me." Groaning softly, he shifted her into position beneath him. "I'm going to work soon."

Sounds faded and colors blurred, then blacked out. They began the slow descent into a black chasm where everything was sensation. Its darkness eclipsed the rest of the world. Consumed by the sudden rush of desire and the ever-increasing hunger that went with it, she answered the message of his lips and encroaching hunger of his body.

Alex checked the clock on the dashboard of his car; he was running late. Not only was he running late, he was tired. A smile curved his lips—he didn't have to ask himself why. He had made Sara his; she was back in his life, back in his arms. That only left back in his bed. For the time being he had to settle for getting into hers. He reached for a cigarette and lit it, inhaling deeply as he waited for the light to change.

It had been better than expected, he told himself with cold, calculating assessment. He would give her that. There was no woman who could turn him on the way she could. That was a fact. A warning voice inside his head told him to stay cool or she was going to walk all over his feelings again. That was the danger with Sara; she touched some deep sensitive chord inside him. He had to steel himself against it. While he was playing the role of seducer, thinking how good he was at it, how great it was going to feel when Raphael lost his head and started making mistakes, he found it all too easy to say things to Sara that made him pause to examine his own words. Last night in the heat of the moment he had said, *"Mi querida perdida."* Was he really only playing a role to get what he wanted when he spoke those words, or were the feelings slipping out, coming straight from the heart, instead of from his hard head?

The dizzying realization that she had fallen hopelessly in love with Alex all over again, even more so than when she was nineteen, followed Sara around for the next few days. All the symptoms of being in love were there. The distraction, the continuous breaks in concentration, the counting of the hours as she waited to see him again, along with all the nagging doubts about where they would go from here. This time *was* even better, as he had said it would be. But this time had something in common with the first time they had been together. Sara wasn't any more sure of what Alex felt now than she had been the first time around. In

spite of all his overt attention and obvious desire to be
with her, Alex still withheld that enigmatic part of
him. It made her uneasy, but there was no going back
now; the heady threshold of physical passion had been
crossed again. From now on they would be together
wherever and whenever they could.

One time he had said he couldn't keep his hands off
her, but it was equally true for her. She couldn't keep
her hands off him. She wanted him all the time. But it
didn't end there. It wasn't just the physical side of their
relationship that made her want to be with him. She
loved all of Alex—the sharp-edged humor, the volatile temperament, the lazy warmth and the swift perceptive intelligence that lay behind it all. She liked a
man with a lust for life, the vitality and wit that went
with it.

She spent the next few days on some high-flying
plane of happiness. She ate when she thought of it,
slept only when exhausted, and looked forward continually for the next time they could be together. They
met for lunch whenever their schedules allowed. Alex
came over after work, not leaving until the early hours
of the morning or not leaving at all and going to work
from her place in the morning. Her world now re-
volved around Alex. Her sister accepted the situation
with a knowing smile, adding that she always knew
they would get back together.

Raphael had been relegated to the back of Sara's
mind until one evening at home she picked up the
phone absentmindedly, and his velvet accented voice
slipping out of the receiver jolted her back to reality.
She had been ignoring his messages uncertain as to
what to do about them.

"Sara, where have you been? Every time I've tried to reach you, I got your answering machine. Have you been out of town?"

The truth was she had been avoiding him, buying some time for herself. She felt uneasy about telling him that she was seeing Alex again and that she didn't want to see anyone else. After what had happened on the cruise, and after Alex's accusations about Raphael setting him up for the corruption charge, she was understandably edgy about confronting him with the news that she was in love with Alex and wasn't going to be seeing anyone else. Yet she had to tell him; she couldn't avoid him forever.

"I've been working hard on a special photo essay," she said, dragging up the first excuse that came into her head.

"Can we have dinner together?"

"Yes, of course, I'd love that," she murmured.

"What about tomorrow night at The Veranda?" For a long moment she didn't know what to say. There was a pregnant pause, then she remembered Alex saying that he would be working late.

"Is something wrong, Sara?"

Running her hand through her hair, she shifted position, tilting her head downward as she spoke into the receiver. "No, nothing's wrong. That sounds wonderful."

"Good, I'll pick you up at eight." His brusque response told her that he guessed she had been avoiding him.

She put down the phone, closing her eyes. He was shrewd, quick on the uptake; he knew something was going on. A sense of guilt surged inside her as if she had been deceitful, yet she didn't know why. Was it deceitful to fall in love with someone else? There had been no promises made to him, no promises broken. But the intensifying rivalry between the two men, coupled with the knowledge that she played a key role in that rivalry, was the source of her uneasy conscience.

Alex was back working in the Narcotics Division. He and Centac had been cleared by both boards of inquiry and had come through miraculously unscathed. After all the furor had died down, Alex still held the unshakable conviction that it was Raphael who had set him up. Sara had never been convinced, but feeling the way she did about Alex, she never made any reference to the feelings she still clung to regarding her old friend. But now she had to tell Raphael the truth about Alex and their relationship. She didn't want to do it over the telephone. She wanted to let him down gently so that there would be no more nasty repercussions between the three of them—if that was possible.

In a tomato-red figure-hugging dress with a V neckline and long tight-fitting sleeves, Sara was getting ready for her date with Raphael. She was balancing on one foot, hastily slipping on a pump, when the doorbell buzzed sharply several times. Straightening slowly she paused to push her hair away from her face, then turned to check the clock. Raphael was early.

"Be right there!" she shouted as she searched for some slender gold hoop earrings on the dressing room vanity unit. Walking slowly to the front door of the condo fixing one earring in her ear, she prepared herself mentally, composing her features into a pleasant expression. The first five minutes were always important in getting off on the right foot; she wanted to ease into the necessary conversation gently at dinner, not plunge into it right away.

She opened the door expecting to see Raphael's broad smile, but it was Alex's skimming gaze that met her eyes. She froze. Alex had told her he was working late—what was he doing here?

It was obvious that she was dressed for a date. His relaxed stance altered, turning rigid. He moved inside, closing the door behind him.

"Going somewhere, Sara?" he challenged, then propped his hands on his hips, exposing the badge clipped to his pocket, the shoulder holster, all signs of the detective on duty. He was faintly menacing.

She fended off his question casually. "I'm going out to dinner with a friend."

His eyes closed briefly as he smiled to himself, obviously savoring her attempt to elude him when all his street-sharpened senses told him instantly what she was doing. "Is this with one of your *good friends?*"

"What other kind of friend is there?" She was glib, swinging away on the pretense of fixing the other golden hoop in her ear when she really wanted to avoid those all-knowing eyes.

He jerked her suddenly around. "Don't play games with me, Sara."

Knowing it was useless to lie to him, she confessed. "All right, I'm going to dinner with Raphael. I have to tell him about *us.*"

"Just like that. You're going to dinner with Raphael." The smile that wasn't a smile remained on his handsome face, his eyes glittering dangerously. *"Why!"* he barked at her. The word was like a hard slap in the face.

"Because he asked me, and because I have to tell him about us."

Without a word he strode over to the telephone on the desk and snatched the receiver from the cradle. Darkly volatile whenever he felt his goals threatened, Alex issued laconic instructions that sounded more like commands.

"You see this?"

"Of course I see it. Do you think I'm blind!" she scoffed.

"This is a telephone? You punch in the number here, a voice comes out here." He jabbed his finger at both her and the phone. "You tell him, Sara, that you're not going to see him anymore. You are only seeing me. Then you say adios. You put the phone down. It's very simple, nothing complicated about it."

"It's also cold and inhuman," she cried.

Alex turned his head sideways, focusing on some distant point in space. He was coming to the end of a very short rope. He narrowed his eyes. "Sara, you *know* what I told you about him. Yet you go behind my back to see him. I don't want him around you."

"Yes, I *know* what you told me about him. I know how he feels about you. But he also happens to be an old friend, someone I still care about. I don't care what you say—I'm going to tell him in my own way. I owe him that, Alex, because of the past. Hopefully this way things won't escalate any more than they already have between you two. Can't you see that?"

For a fleeting moment something in him relented...a little, so she reinforced her position. "This is the best way for everyone concerned. My way. I'm going."

He stared at her for a long sizzling moment as he measured perhaps what it would cost him to use persuasion to force her to do otherwise. Something checked him. Regrouping his thoughts, he let his gaze drop to the dress she was wearing, surveying it slowly inch by inch. His eyes hardened. "Okay, you go, but not dressed like that."

"What!"

"You heard me. You don't go in the dress you're wearing. We are going to find something else for you to wear." His brusque manner took charge, telling her that by *we* he meant *I,* inflaming her own considerable temper.

"What's wrong with this dress?"

"It shows off everything," he snapped, grimly waving his hand with a dismissive gesture. Before she could issue a retort he had his hand on the small of her back, propelling her toward the bedroom—a path he knew well. Inside the bedroom she took up a position near the closet, folding her arms in front of her as he riffled through her clothes.

"Find anything? I hear yellow is really big this year." She batted her eyelashes and he shot her a dry look, then his hand stopped when he came to a Swiss polka-dot white dress that buttoned up to the neck. Yanking it out with a satisfied expression, he tossed it at her. As their eyes dueled silently, she caught the dress.

"He'll love you in that."

"Do you realize how utterly ridiculous this is? If you don't think you can trust me, what are we doing getting involved?"

He moved around her and hovered in back of her. "I'm protecting what belongs to me."

Suddenly the zipper went flying down her back with a searing sound. The red dress parted, cool air caressing the satin skin of her bare back.

"He's going to be here any minute," she snapped. "Will you please leave before he arrives?"

Pushing the red dress down her arms, she stepped out of it, then flung it onto the bed. In lacy demi bra and revealing bikini panties, she stood quivering inwardly with rage. She observed his gaze sliding appreciatively over what he considered belonged to him.

"Maybe you want him to find you here," she challenged. "Maybe you want to see this whole situation blow up in your face."

"Where are you going tonight?" he asked, suddenly serious.

"The Veranda. It's a very nice restaurant."

He moved close to her, watching her slip on the white dress. "Don't change that dress after I go. I have lots of friends all around Miami," he announced in a low, intimate, teasing tone.

She clenched her eyes with rising frustration, knowing Raphael would be arriving. "Stop hovering and go!"

"I'm going. But I would like to stay and *hover* over you," he retorted, amused. His good humor had returned now that he had come out on top. His hand caught the curve of her neck, and slanting his head, he planted a hard kiss of possession on her mouth. She swayed toward him, melting. When he backed away there was a very satisfied look in his eyes.

Raphael sat opposite her, his dark wavy hair shining under the recessed lighting, the ever-present glint of amusement in his dark eyes and the wide smile curving his mouth. They had been catching up on things, enjoying a predinner drink at the restaurant's bar and listening to the live jazz band. For a moment Raphael studied his glass, and she sensed what was coming.

"I have a feeling that you have been avoiding me. Did what happened on the cruise between me and Cordera make you change your mind about me? I know how it must have looked. We both got very aggressive, but . . . I didn't think it would affect the way you feel about me as a friend."

She had no desire to see him grovel, to see him brought down by her attitude toward him. There was still a part of her heart that belonged to the past, and he was part of that past. She knew the moment had come to tell him about Alex and her.

Looking down at her glass, she said, "There's something I should tell you." She lifted her gaze and met his thoughtful one steadily. "Alex and I have started seeing each other again."

Her words had a powerful effect. For a few fleeting seconds he was absolutely still. She scanned the proud strong features of his magnificently controlled face. His dark, usually smiling eyes dulled, then went blank, as if a light had been switched off somewhere in his head.

At the look in his eyes she rushed on. "I know I gave the impression that Alex and I were never very serious about each other. But the truth is, we were. Since I came back to Miami the attraction between him and me has become very much alive. In fact, very strong." She reached out to touch his hand. "Raphael, from now on I don't think I'll be seeing anyone else."

She watched him, feeling like the lowest thing on earth.

Then he drew on those inner reserves that his background and strong will provided. "So this is the way it has to be?"

"Yes," she said quietly, not avoiding his eyes.

"I am very sorry that it is not me you feel this way about. I am selfish. I wanted you for myself. But I am not so selfish that I don't wish for your happiness. You mean too much to me for that." His hands reached out to engulf hers, raising one to his lips while his eyes conveyed the sincerity of his message. She found his reaction very moving.

The broad smile returned, slowly illuminating his face. The atmosphere lightened between them. She felt herself relaxing imperceptibly. His head shot up when the waiter appeared to tell them their table was ready. They rose from the bar stool and followed the waiter into the dining room where he stood by their table to take their orders. By the time they were alone, Raphael's natural ebullience had returned as if it had never deserted him.

Had she dramatized the whole situation in her mind, blown it out of proportion? For a moment she felt foolish. Then she remembered the vitriolic aggression between Alex and Raphael on board the yacht. No, she had not overdramatized that. But Raphael's reaction now was so magnanimous that Alex's warnings, the vagueness of Raphael's responses to her queries about his business associations and the confidential file, paled into insignificance. She wished Alex could see the Raphael whom she knew, but she doubted it would make any difference.

The rest of the evening sped by as they enjoyed each other's company, even ending on a high note. At the door to her condo he insisted on kissing her goodnight. The kiss was restrained, respectful of the choice she had made. Then he was gone. Sara felt only a deep inner peace as she watch him slide into his car. Everything had worked out all right, after all. She was glad she had done things her way.

The following evening Alex kept firing questions at Sara as they drove in his car to have dinner with another couple. The questions were all about her date with Raphael. She was being grilled.

"How did he react when you told him that from now on you were with me?"

The words Alex chose were ones Raphael had issued on the yacht. She sliced a sideways look at him as she answered, "He was magnanimous and warm. In other words, my happiness mattered more to him than any negative feelings he had for you. I wish you could know him the way I know him," she murmured.

"Yeah, I'm sure I would be very impressed." Alex shot her a sarcastic glance that told her she was wasting her time and breath, so she let the subject drop and concentrated on the passing scenery.

"Did this magnanimity include a good-night kiss by any chance?"

"A very tender, goodbye kiss."

"You mean he didn't try to leave you with something to remember him by?"

"This conversation is pointless, Alex. You don't believe anything I say, so why do you keep asking?" She concentrated on the scenery again, then wisely changed the topic of conversation.

They met Alex's friends at a restaurant and then went on to see a film. After the film they all went for a drink, then Alex took her home. Parked outside the condo, Alex switched off the engine and turned to her in the shadows of the car. He leaned forward, so that only inches separated them, then his lips caressed the side of her face, taking little nibbling bites along the curve of her neck. She began to melt; her head lolled back against the headrest. Few preliminaries were needed for swift arousal. But Alex lifted his head, checking himself, his burning gaze absorbing hers.

"Aren't you coming in?" Her tone was low and intimate. There was no mistaking the invitation implied in the softly spoken words.

His eyes darkened with pleasure. "Tonight I want you to come with me."

"What do you mean?" Sara knew the invitation heralded some kind of maneuver.

A smile deepened the grooves around his mouth. His gaze slid down to the deep plunge of the V-necked red dress—the one he had insisted she not wear for Raphael but then insisted she wear for him—back up to her lips, absorbing every physical detail about her.

"It's happening all over again just like seven years ago. Isn't it, Sara?" The smoothness of his tone, the primitive male possession in his eyes turned her thighs to jelly.

"What are you saying?" she murmured.

One of his fingers traced the neckline of her dress and rested in the shadowy cleft. "I'm not satisfied," he announced quietly. "That's what I'm saying." The words jumped between them, leaping into a heavy pool of silence.

"But we've been seeing a lot of each other," she murmured momentarily perplexed by what he meant.

"But it's not enough." He lifted his hand from her neck and sank it into her hair; he pulled at it with a tender tug. Grudging desire lit his eyes. For the first time in weeks she realized there were still conflicting feelings inside him.

"You've really got me hooked this time, Sara. It's worse than last time." A look of charged reluctance accompanied the admission, but quickly passed and he continued. "I want you to live with me or for us to get a place together. I'm tired of sneaking in and out of the condo at night. I want you with me without your sister hanging around, never knowing when she might walk in on us. I'm tired of wanting you in the middle of the night and not finding you there beside me. When I come in at night from work I want to find you there. When I wake up in the morning I want to see you there asleep next to me."

There was no mention of commitment, for all the burning possession in his eyes; he wasn't asking her to marry him, she could see that. In a way she was relieved; there was still a wariness between them, too many uncertainties that hadn't been settled or explored.

"You mean you want us to live together, no strings attached?" she said hesitantly, making sure she understood him.

"For the time being, that's what I mean," he announced thoughtfully. Lowering his head to the side of her face, so that she couldn't see his expression, he moved his lips against her cheek. "What's your answer?" He prompted her by nipping the soft curve of her neck with his teeth. His hand slid into the plunging neckline of her dress, capturing the warm swell of her breast. His vitality and strength made her eyes close under the assault.

"I'll think it over," she answered softly, shuddering under her own desire, knowing she had already made up her mind.

Sara looked around at the apartment. It was immaculate. Walking through the rooms with Alex, she realized it was even nicer than she had thought after their first hurried look the night before. The owner was a very good friend of Alex, who had gone to work in Europe. Alex had phoned him and everything had been arranged for them to use it on a temporary basis. They had decided to move into a new place rather than use Alex's condo because it was neutral ground, a meeting of the ways.

This apartment was beautiful, fully furnished, and they were lucky to get it. It was an airy retreat with graceful arched ceilings and doors that opened onto small flower-choked balconies with terrazzo floors that gleamed in the sunlight; the balconies looked down on a small brick courtyard where night-blooming jasmine grew. The uncarpeted areas were cool and spacious. Thick chocolate-colored carpeting and umber leather sofa and chairs gave the living room an arresting sobriety. Recessed lighting and discreet touches of brass added warmth.

Sara stood in the middle of the living room, turning slowly around, delighted with the place. Alex caught her. "Come this way. There's something I want to show you." He took her hand, leading her down a short hallway, giving her the history of the building. The block of condos had been built in the 1930s and was on the edge of the Art Deco district in Miami Beach. He led her into the kitchen, where she admired the black-and-white mosaic floor and old-fashioned cupboards.

"Wouldn't you just know a macho man would lead a woman to the kitchen?"

He quirked an inquiring eyebrow. "Have you learned how to cook yet? You didn't know one end of a saucepan from the other when you were nineteen." He dropped his tone to one of intimate conspiracy. "Love and food are very closely associated in the human mind. So if you love me you have to cook for me."

"Who ever said anything about loving you?" she teased in a soft husky voice. "I'm only here because you're great in the sack." They looked at each other in the sizzling moment. The word *love* had never been used between them, yet it was all around them.

"In that case let's take another look at the bedroom." With his arm linked around her he guided her back through the hallway into the master bedroom.

Sara went around opening closets and drawers. He pulled her inside the adjoining bathroom.

"The shower looks big enough for us both. If I had the time we could try it out." They were both getting a strong sense of déjà vu, an intoxicating, arousing, chilling memory of a steamy encounter in another time and another condo.

He moved closer. Her hands rested on his shoulders as he leaned forward and captured her mouth with a kiss that was hotly passionate as if he were finally taking complete possession of her, rather than a piece of real estate. Her mouth parted under the demanding pressure of his; the kiss was long, searching and hungry. They swayed back against the counter of the vanity unit. When he broke off the kiss there was a disturbed edge to his breathing. His hands ran up and down her bare arms in a rough caressing movement that reflected his reluctance to stop what he had initiated.

"I've got to get back to work," he announced, moving his lips against her forehead. "See you tonight." He put her gently away, then reached into his pocket and pulled out some keys to the condo.

"Here—I had several sets made up, one for each of us and some spares."

Her fingers closed around the keys. The cold metal felt alien. For a moment she stared down at them. When she looked up again, he was studying her with an abstracted absorption that charged the moment with significance. Still watching her, he reached into his pocket a second time, pulling out a money clip, to peel off some bills.

"Here's some money, to buy food or anything else you need around here." A flush crept across her face. Never had she been more conscious of her status than at that moment. It was as if he had rented her along with the condo.

"I don't like this, Alex," she said, meeting his eyes.

"Forget it. We're starting over. Give it a chance, Sara. We'll move away from this. It's only temporary."

If they were together, if they were putting the past behind them, if they were starting fresh, if they wanted only to be together, why had they both shied back from any mention of commitment? she wondered. The question hung unspoken in the air between them. It was an undeniable fact that neither of them had mentioned the future. Neither of them was ready yet to take that blind leap of faith into the dark, into the unknown. They were testing the water before they plunged in completely again. For the time being this was the arrangement. That was the unspoken message in his eyes. Alex still didn't trust her one hundred percent. He wanted her, though. He'd made that very plain.

He adjusted his tie. "I'm out of here. I'll see you tonight." He kissed her on the cheek, a kiss completely different from the one that had preceeded it. For a moment he surveyed her. "Everything okay, Sara?"

"Everything's fine." She smiled slowly.

"The last time you said everything was fine I didn't see you for seven years." A wide teasing smile accompanied his words. "Don't go taking off without a word this time." Silently she watched him back toward the door. He bounced his car keys in the palm of his hand, never missing a beat. "Okay?"

"I won't," she said quietly. "What about you?"

"I'm not going anywhere," he concluded with an enigmatic smile. Then he was gone.

Chapter 7

It didn't take Sara long to grow accustomed to her new surroundings or the intimacy of her new life-style with Alex. She thrived on that part of it. But she also had to accustom herself to Alex's heavy working schedule; she soon learned that he didn't like to talk about his work or bring it home with him. When he did come home it was usually very late. But nothing could mar the glow of her happiness. It spilled over into everything she did, adding a new dimension to her sense of well-being.

She wasn't the only one deeply affected. Alex was, too. Occasionally she would catch him looking at her as if he were seeing her for the first time, studying her with an intensity that unnerved her. It was as if she had glimpsed a ruthless streak in his nature. When he saw the effect this had on her, he would immediately turn to acting the warm, smooth macho rogue, teasing her with a lazy sense of sharp-edged humor and his passionate Cuban nature. But he couldn't disguise the fact that he liked having her around. It was there in his eyes when he walked into the kitchen in the morning to find her making coffee or preparing breakfast. It was there in his eyes again when he got home late from work and found her somewhere in the condo. Sara felt as though she were hopelessly addicted to him.

Besides the intimacy there were also all the other things they did together, places they liked to go, people they liked to see, who amused or interested them. But in spite of all this Sara was still troubled by how Alex kept a large chunk of himself submerged; he never talked about how he felt or what he did during the day. When she casually questioned him about his work or attempted to draw him out on the subject it was as if a door closed in her face.

There were also two highly sensitive topics they both did their best to avoid and never talked about at all—one was the past and the other was Raphael Cruzero. Apart from those exceptions, the days flew by, happily tinged with the uncertainty of what lay ahead, but heady and satisfying and absorbing all the same.

They had been living together for three months, Sara realized as she looked at the calendar on her desk in the newsroom. Enjoying a cup of steaming coffee, she glanced to the windows. It was March, and the undiluted brilliant sunshine of Florida's sunny warm winter attracted people in droves—it was the height of the season.

But the newsroom was in the doldrums. She gazed across its wide expanse, filled with desks and computers, lit with long strips of fluorescent lighting. The offices of editors surrounded the open pool of desks for the copy writers, feature writers, reporters and photographers. The desks were littered with phones, coffee cups, personal memorabilia, pens and correspondence.

Her telephone buzzed; she was perched on the edge of the desk, so she put down her coffee cup and reached over languidly to answer it. Lately her job had begun to pall, she thought, lifting the receiver to her ear. Exciting stories were far and few between. When the news was dull, so was the photography. She wasn't surprised to hear James Bailey, a magazine editor, getting back to her. Bored, she had begun to look into doing some free-lance photography on the side.

But what he had to say came as a surprise, a more than welcome one. "Sara, we're in a bind over here. One of our best staff photographers was supposed to cover Carnival in Brazil for us. Well he's been in a skiing accident and broke his leg. I know it's short notice, but is there any possibility you could cover this assignment for us . . . ?"

As he continued, her outlook changed dramatically. She found herself virtually hanging on to each word. She couldn't believe her ears. They wanted to do a six-page spread on Carnival in Brazil. It was something she had always secretly dreamed of doing. The editor sounded desperate. They needed someone with experience and preferably an intimate knowledge of the South American continent. With her background at *Photographic* and the years she'd spent growing up there, he thought she could do a first-rate job.

"The only problem, Sara, is can you get away?"

"I'm almost certain I can," she explained. "I can take some of the vacation time I've got coming to me." Sara would have crawled on her hands and knees to get this assignment. Her creative juices were already flowing like a heady stream, excitement firing her imagination. She had never seen the color and excesses of Carnival; that week of unbridled hedonistic pleasure before the Lenten season was something her parents thought children should not be exposed to.

"I'll talk with my editor here and see if I can get some time off," she murmured. "I'll call you back as soon as possible. What about tomorrow?"

"I have to have a decision today. The sooner the better. We're in a bind, and I've got one other person in mind besides you. But I called you first. Sara, the seat is booked. I have the tickets lying in front of me on my desk. I have to notify the airline of the change in name, that's all. Officially Carnival starts on Saturday and continues until Ash Wednesday. But we'd like to get someone in there by Friday night. Is your passport up to date?"

"Yes, of course. All I have to do is make arrangements with the director of photography, and throw a few things in a bag." She was an old hand at packing at the drop of a hat. Clothes were kept to a minimum; her camera gear made up the bulk of her baggage.

"I'll be waiting for you to get back to me."

The *Guardian*'s head of photography was flexible and agreed that since she had some vacation time coming she could use part of it for this trip. They worked out a few more details and reached an agreement. Buoyed up with anticipation Sara drove back to the condo, looking forward to this assignment with more enthusiasm than anything she had run across since joining the newspaper staff months ago.

That evening Sara explored the hall closet to find where Alex had stored her suitcases. She carried one into the bedroom and packed, keeping in mind that the weather in Brazil would be steamy since it was summer there. She carefully packed her camera gear, making sure everything was there—the expensive range of lenses, the filters, camera bodies, turbo flash attachment and light meter. She had just zipped up the suitcase when she heard Alex coming through the door. She looked at the clock. He seemed to be getting back later and later in the evening.

Walking slowly into the living room to greet him, she smiled widely at him. His appearance always triggered a big smile, but tonight the trip to Brazil spurred it on and it had extra dazzle.

"Hi," she called out to him. She linked her arms around his neck and brushed her lips against the side of his mouth. He stood there, accepting her overtures of affection as if they were his just due, appearing for the moment to be unaffected. Then his hands tightened in response. With natural wary male reserve, he assessed her extraordinary good mood.

"Had a good day?" he inquired softly.

"Hmm, yes." She smiled mysteriously. Then she focused on the lines of fatigue around his eyes and mouth and she frowned, forgetting about the trip to Brazil for a moment. Twelve- and fourteen-hour days were typical for Alex.

"Why are you working so many hours? Do you really have to work this hard, Alex?"

"If we want to get what we go after, we have to put in the hours." He shrugged as if it were of no consequence. That was all he would divulge; his expression became shuttered and he put her gently away from him. He headed into the kitchen, opened the refrigerator door to get a lager and flipped off the cap. He didn't bother with a glass, and tilting his head back, he closed his eyes and savored the first swallow. When he opened them again, his gaze followed her speculatively.

Sara walked over to the kitchen counter and leaned against it, crossing one bare leg over the other. His eyes swept over her, trailing down the bared leg, exposed by the slit of the robe she was wearing.

A casserole was heating in the microwave, wafting out a tantalizing aroma. It was the most satisfactory solution she had discovered for solving the problem of planning meals when his hours were so long and so erratic.

"So how is the lady of my life? What's she been up to?" With his street-smart eyes Sara could do little that escaped him.

She smiled with tantalizing charm. She linked her arms around his neck again. Tossing her long hair away from her face, she tilted her head backward at a beguiling angle and came clean.

"The editor from a travel magazine telephoned me today. Some time ago I contacted him and showed him a portfolio of work I did for *World Photographic* and told him I was interested in doing some free-lance work. We had a nice long talk and he said he'd get back to me if anything came up."

"So... what's so great about that?" Leaning back against the snack bar, he put down the lager. He locked his hands on her slim waist and drew her between his legs, regarding her with lazy possession and an amiable warmth in his eyes. An air of mild curiosity hung around him.

"The staff photographer who had this assignment has been in a skiing accident and broke his leg. The editor, James Bailey, is in a real bind. They need another photographer right away to take the photographer's place. He wants me to take it. It's Brazil at Carnival time. I've always dreamed of getting this assignment. They say Carnival has to be seen to be believed. It's got everything—color, intense energy, wild exuberance, visual spectacle, sensual excesses—no one *sleeps* for four nights during Carnival. I'll be exhausted when I get back, but I know I'm going to love every minute. Most likely I'll do some of the best work I've ever done."

She watched the warmth vanish from his expression. He didn't look even remotely impressed by what she was saying or by her enthusiasm.

"What's the matter?" she asked.

"I don't like it. That's what's the matter."

"What don't you like about it?"

Alex's steady gaze locked onto hers. He removed her arms from around his neck with the air of a man searching for an excuse when he really didn't have a good one to justify what he was feeling, or a man who didn't want to admit what he was feeling. He put her away from him and not too gently. "Do I have to give a reason? Can't you just accept that I don't want you to do something?"

"Yes. You have to give a reason. I want to hear a reasonable explanation."

"All right." He sliced the air with his hand in a gesture of exasperation. "I've heard about Brazil, at Carnival time, the 'anything goes' atmosphere."

This she could understand; it almost made her smile. But the look in his eyes told her it was better not to. "Relax, Alex. I'm not going to peel off my clothes and dance the samba half-naked through the streets. I'm going to be working flat out. You've got nothing to worry about." She laughed softly and reached up to pat his jaw affectionately with her hand.

He smiled back at her for a reassuring moment, and when he spoke his voice was like a soft caress. "I'm not going to worry. You're right about that, Sara, because you're not going."

For a moment she could do nothing but stare in mute astonishment. The look in his eyes told her his Latin temperament was revving up.

Hooking one leg on a snack bar stool, he dragged it forward and sank onto it. Sara watched him in stony silence.

"Let's go back over this for a moment, okay? An editor calls you up with an assignment to go to Brazil. I walk in here and you don't ask me or talk it over with me, you *tell* me you're going." By the time he finished the last phrase his voice was a low roar.

"It was a last-minute thing, Alex. I had to give him an answer right away or he would have moved on to someone else," she explained.

"Then maybe you should have said no, Sara. Did you ever think of saying no?"

Once again she stared at him in mute disbelief. "I must be pretty thick because it never occurred to me that I *had* to talk it over with you, that I had to ask you anything. You don't talk anything over with me. You don't even tell me anything about what you do all day long. You don't tell me what you feel or what you're thinking."

Closing his eyes, his forbearance strained to the limit, he replied, "Sara, you know and I know that I can't pick and choose my assignments. I have a job to do. It's not free-lance."

"Well, I can pick and choose. I want this assignment. They don't come any juicier than this. Besides, you have no right to interfere or to try and stop me."

He smiled at her, a smile that said he was about to explode. "Let me make sure I've got this right. We are lovers. We sleep in the same bed. We live under the same roof. But you're saying—" he jabbed his finger at her "—you're saying I have nothing to say about what you do.

"I'm a man and you are a woman. We are together. That gives me a say in what you do and what you don't do." They stared at each other for a long sizzling moment. "Take pictures around here," he roared.

"Take pictures around here?" she scoffed, rolling her eyes to the ceiling. "You make it sound like I'm running around shooting snapshots for the family album. This is what I do for a living—this is what I do best. This is what I'm interested in!"

"I thought you were interested in me, Sara," he shot back laconically.

"And I thought you were interested in me. But the only interest you seem to have in me is figuring out how you're going to get me underneath you." She moved away out of the kitchen, but he rose from the stool and caught up with her in two quick strides, hauling her around so that they were face-to-face again. With their noses inches apart he held her locked into place.

"I don't hear any objections when I do." His tone was lazy, but menacing. Sara's face burned with the instant knowledge that he was right; she never refused his advances. They were all welcome, she had a deep craving for them, and at times like this she thought that craving was what was holding them together.

He read the look in her eyes with unerring accuracy. "On that one level we communicate without any trouble, don't we, Sara?" His expression changed to autocratic. "I want you with me, not running around on some other continent. That's why I asked you to move in with me. I thought that was why you were here. Because you wanted to *be* with *me.*"

"It's a four-day assignment, Alex," she pointed out coldly. "Besides, you're hardly ever here. I don't suppose you'll even notice right away I'm gone." As soon as the words were out of her mouth she regretted them. The sensual line of his mouth thinned. His expression grew more intense.

"I was wondering how long it would take for you to get around to throwing that at me, using my long hours for some convenient excuse to take off again." He squeezed the soft skin of her upper arms, then he thrust her away from him.

She stood silently, stunned by the forceful feelings aroused by a simple trip to Brazil. Everything up to now had been so good. Dazed, she listened to him slam out of the condo.

Her lips parted on a soft protest but no words came out. Staring at the closed door, she remained motionless for several long moments. When she heard the car engine turn over in the courtyard outside the condominium block, tears of confusion and frustration stung at her eyes. What on earth was he so mad about? She'd never dreamed he would act like this. She ran a distracted hand through her hair, deciding he had left to cool off. It was better that he did, she concluded.

She walked into their bedroom, but the empty silence only depressed her, so she went back into the spare room to finish packing for the trip. She had given her word to the editor, made arrangements at the newspaper for time off—it was too late to back out now. She was going to Brazil, she thought firmly, snapping shut the lid of the suitcase with an air of resolve.

Alex got out of his car at the beach and walked along, thinking about Sara. Where Sara was concerned, seven years hadn't changed him much. He never could keep a cool head. He was still one volatile Latino.

Nothing illustrated that more than tonight when she had sprung this trip on him without any warning. What lay behind his anger? Why had his temper gone off like a rocket? She had made a decision without even thinking of him. The fact that he was in no position to demand anything from her didn't matter to him. He only knew he didn't like it.

But it went deeper than that. He knew what the real reason was behind his deeper anger. She had trodden on an old wound. The incident reminded him too much of that time she had walked out and left nothing but a four-line note. He was quickly discovering that when she turned her back on him he couldn't be reasonable about it. He had been telling himself for months now that he was just using Sara to get Cruzero. But now he was discovering he wasn't as detached about the situation as he wanted to be.

Chapter 8

When Sara flew to Rio the following day, some of the shine had been taken off the trip. Pensively gazing out the plane's window, she remembered the cool parting this morning as she left for the airport. Alex had not returned home until the early hours of the morning. But she had awakened instantly when he came in, listening in silence to his clothes dropping onto a chair, his shoes hitting the floor, and feeling the bed sink beneath his weight. For the first time since they were reunited they had slept as far away as possible from each other. She felt the coolness coming from his body as he turned his broad back and pulled the sheets around him.

As soon as she arrived in Rio, samba fever put the incident from her mind. Electrified by the energy of the city, she wanted to capture it all on film. Working feverishly, using roll after roll of film, she was like any photographer bombarded with spectacular images. Her concentration was focused and there was little that could break it. The magnificent samba parades that various schools of Rio put on all night at the huge Sambadrome awed her. The exclusive club balls packed by the wealthy, decked out in fantastic, erotic costumes were equally colorful. But the true spirit of Carnival was found in the streets and on the beaches, where people danced through the night. In Brazil Carnival was more a spirit of exhibitionism than out-and-out debauchery, Sara discovered. The skimpy costumes on the streets and beaches were meant to tantalize and fuel the imagination more than anything else. Running on pure adrenaline, she didn't bother about sleep at night but caught up on it during lulls during the day. The four days passed like a wild Technicolor dream, pulsating to throbbing samba rhythms while she strove for those perfect shots.

When she flew out of Rio on Ash Wednesday, the streets were littered and forlorn and she felt utterly exhausted. But it was the satisfying exhaustion that came from a job well done; she had done some of her best work ever. The magazine didn't pay all that much, but the trip paid a huge dividend in creative energy, unsurpassed by any other assignment she could recall.

The images were already beginning to fade when she walked out of Miami International Airport with a sense of deep peace at returning home. The nearer she got to home, the more Alex was on her mind. When she arrived, she wandered slowly through the rooms of the empty condo, searching for signs of Alex's existence. The place was dead without him, but there were signs of him everywhere. In the bedroom his clothes were strewn haphazardly around while the sheets were tangled as if some torturous nightmare had gripped him in sleep. She looked at the bedside clock, wondering where he was. Working impossible hours, socializing with his men after work as usual, she guessed with a sigh. He wouldn't be back for hours yet. She had plenty of time to freshen up.

She changed into a sleeveless white dress that brought out the deep golden tones of her tan from the beaches of Ipanema and Copacabana. Hair sleeked back, golden hoops in her ears, she put finishing touches to her makeup with one eye on the clock. She was hanging things away in the closet when she finally heard the key in the lock. She could feel her face soften with pleasure. Her eyes deepened with molten silver, and she had an irresistible urge to smile.

Controlling a natural eagerness she composed her expression and walked slowly into the living room to greet Alex. His gaze collided instantly with hers when she stood in the doorway. Neither of them could hide the reaction they felt at the sight of the other.

"Hi," she called out softly.

"You decided to come back this time." He shrugged out of his jacket, turning his back to her. Her gaze crawled over him, taking in every inch. While he unbuckled the shoulder harness she walked quietly up behind him. Sliding her arms around his hard waist, she pressed her face into his back, closing her eyes and breathing in his scent.

His powerful frame stiffened as if he was fighting off her and something else inside him every inch of the way. He ignored her until he had put the .38 revolver safely out of the way. Then he turned to confront her.

"I missed you," she said simply.

He loosened his tie and flicked open his shirt collar. His expression said he wasn't buying her statement. It warned her to keep her distance, to cool it until his pride came to terms with some conflicting inner emotions he had about her reappearance. Danger lurked behind his deceptive smile.

"*Cuidado, Sara, cuidado,*" he said, holding up his hand in a gesture that warned her away. "I'm tired and not in the best of moods." With macho arrogance he ignored her, turning to walk down the short hallway to the master bedroom. Curiosity motivated her to follow—as well as her visual hunger for him.

"I need a shower. Tonight I feel like an animal." He flicked a lazy eyebrow in her direction. A flash of amusement accompanied the words, reminding her that she had on one memorable occasion called him an overheated primate. He pulled off his shirt with impatience and stripped off the rest of his clothes, tossing them onto a nearby chair.

She studied his broad, muscular back, riveted by the fascinating play of muscles and shoulder blades, by the lean male flanks and long hard legs. Animal or no animal he wasn't ready to welcome her back—that was pretty clear, she thought—slightly amused. The mighty Cuban was either still sulking or frustrated and fed up from working hard on a case and getting nowhere. She adopted a wait-and-see attitude. The shower went on full blast, hitting the tiled walls like needles.

"Has some part of the investigation you're working on gone wrong?" she asked over the roar of the water.

"I don't feel like talking about it, Sara," he shouted back.

She moved away, then turned back. She stood in the bathroom doorway, wondering why he was always so closemouthed about his work. He never told her how he felt about anything, she thought again. They enjoyed themselves when they went out and socialized, they spent time together, but a part of him shut her out. She was beginning to resent it.

"It's good to talk about things, you know. Why don't you ever want to talk about your work? I thought men enjoyed talking about what they do," she murmured when she heard the water finally stop.

The shower door slid back sharply. Alex emerged, water streaming down his powerful body. As he reached for a towel, his burnt sienna eyes pinned her. "Have we got some kind of communication gap here tonight? When I say I don't feel like talking about it, that's what I mean. I don't feel like talking about it."

She watched him hook the towel around his hips, then pick up another to dry his hair. He was being deliberately obnoxious. Her own temper was slowly unraveling.

"Want to go out and get something to eat?"

He eyed her steadily, then challenged with another suggestion. "I don't want to go out and eat, Sara. I have a better idea. Why don't you fix me something?"

It was not a straightforward request; it was one of his arrogant macho demands to see what she would do next. They stared at each other. If he had been a little more pleasant she would have been happy to fix something for him. But he was trying to make her feel as though she had done something wrong by going to Brazil, and Sara didn't see things that way. He was needling her and she wasn't going to let him get away with it.

"Why don't you fix *yourself* something? It will be a new experience for you. A little walk on the wild side. The kitchen is that way. It's the room with the sink and the table in it."

"Meanness and a smart mouth, so much in one woman. I'm a lucky guy." Alex wielded his sharp-edged humor like a sword.

Ignoring him, she walked back into the bedroom and unzipped the white dress. Stepping out of it, she hung it in the closet, yanked her hair loose from its sleek moorings, and grabbed a brush, then sank onto the bed, trying to batten down her ruffled feelings. He was being unreasonable, completely unreasonable. She shot the brush through her hair, which crackled with electricity. She looked up to see Alex gazing at her as if seeing her for the first time. Tiny beads of moisture from the shower still gleamed on his skin. A silver medallion hung from a thick chain around his neck. While his arms were occupied drying his thick hair, his pectoral muscles flexed. Raw masculinity poured from him. The hairbrush stilled in her hand.

He said nothing, just flung the towel viciously aside as if he had had just about enough with some battle inside himself. He looked from her eyes to the narrow straps holding up her creamy satin lace slip which contrasted with her tanned skin. His fist punched the wall switch, and darkness enveloped the room. Her eyes followed him like a cat's in the dark until his shadowy impressive form loomed over her.

He clamped his hands on the soft skin of her shoulders. "I'm not taking second place to any damn camera, Sara. Let's get that straight. As long as you're with me, I come number-one in your life."

"Don't touch me."

"What's the matter? You missed me, didn't you? I'm going to give you the chance to show me how much. Or maybe you would rather go to bed with your camera."

"Maybe you would like to to to bed with your gun," she retaliated.

"That wouldn't be true for either of us. You're the only one who satisfies me." He shook her with a kind of tender violence. "But you want me, too. No one else satisfies you. We suffer from the same disease."

"Why don't we ever talk about things?"

"We did talk things over." The smile in his expression and tone didn't mask the steel behind his words. "Remember, I wanted you here. You wanted to go. Doesn't that bring back memories? Doesn't that remind you of something in the past?"

Her palms flattened on the heated rock-hard surface of his skin, but it was like pushing against an oncoming truck. When his mouth found hers, she let out a low tortured moan of want mingled with protest until he broke off the kiss and lifted his head.

"What was it like down in Brazil? Did you see lots of good-looking guys?" His eyes burned into hers; he was the quintessential jealous man.

"When I get wrapped up in my work I don't think about anything else. And when I was finished I only wanted to get back here to be with you. You *are* number-one in my life."

"Maybe." He paused, looking at her for long disturbing moments. Satisfied momentarily, he lowered his head and kissed her with rough tenderness, like a man trying to batten down the hard passion that burned within him but not succeeding.

Lifting her to a kneeling position, he pushed the straps of the slip down her arms. Watching the full swell of her breasts slowly emerge, he buried his face between them, locking his powerful arms around her hips. She shuddered with pleasure, rested her palms on his shoulders near his neck, then sank her fingers into his hair, clutching his head to her breast. In moments he had her pinned beneath his weight. Whispered words of passion passed between them, all mixed together like their feelings for each other. It didn't matter that some of his words were in another language; they needed no translation.

Kissing her deeply Alex wasted no time on preliminaries. He made love like a man who had been in prison. He was rough and possessive, arousing her rapidly. To Sara it was as if he wanted to reestablish a claim that had been challenged, reasserting his ownership, his domination, his possession.

Their desire for each other was like a shimmering fierce heat as they scaled the walls of pleasure together climbing the exquisite, almost unbearable, heights. Groaning low in his throat he took what she offered and still demanded more, as if tonight nothing would satisfy him but total possession of mind and body. Breathing heavily in her ear, he drew her leg over his hip and ground his pleasure into hers, bringing them both to an intense quick physical crisis. They lay back in a pool of sated pleasure, the minutes passing slowly until the banked fires glowed again, fanned back to life by the need accumulated during days apart from each other. He made love to her again, locking his hands beneath her hips, whispering low commands, his voice thickening with arousal.

When Alex finally rolled away, his breathing was harsh and labored, echoing some kind of discordancy that remained between them. They had both been satisfied physically but only for the present. There was a chink in the bond that welded them together, a mental gap that had to be bridged, and they both knew they hadn't crossed it.

He waited for Sara to fall asleep. She lay flat on her stomach, her face pressed into the pillow. He sat up and reached for a cigarette. The flame of the lighter glowed in the dark, illuminating part of Sara's face. His head lolled back into the pillows.

He began thinking of the times after his parents came over from Cuba, when they had to leave everything behind. They had to start all over again from scratch, with nothing. It had been hard on the whole family. In Cuba his father had been prominent in local government. They had all been used to the luxuries of a more affluent life-style: ballet lessons for his sister, domestic help around the house. It was a completely different way of life when they came to the States. They all had to grow up fast in a harsh world with no frills. His parents were away working long hours at menial jobs just to ensure there was a roof over their heads and food on the table.

He remembered those days all too well, he thought ruefully. He was always in some kind of trouble in school. Maybe he hadn't been exactly bad, but for a while he had been headed in the wrong direction. Some people said inside every cop there was a re-formed criminal. He didn't believe that, but there was a kernel of truth in it somewhere for him. Better times had turned him around, but he'd never forgotten those bad days. The home he had grown up in was empty and cold, so he had hung around in the streets. It had been like that when Sara walked out on him, the same kind of feeling. The warmth had gone out of his life. He'd hated it. He didn't want Sara to know how he felt. It was something she could exploit and he wanted to keep the upper hand. If he was going to get Rapha-el Cruzero, he had to stay cool and keep the upper hand.

Alex got up when Sara was asleep and walked to the balcony, sliding open the patio door. He leaned on the railing, hands spread apart, gazing into the darkness, listening to the age-old distant rumble of the ocean. He didn't like to admit to himself how much he had missed Sara while she was away, how much her ab-sence had dragged at his sense of well-being. Things were not going exactly the way he had figured they would go. For the second time he had to admit to himself how much a part of his life she had become in such a short period. When he came back to the condo at night during the past four days, there was that strange silence, that emptiness. Missing her had not been part of his plan.

That thought irritated him. He tossed the cigarette away and told himself to forget it. Nothing was going to get in his way; he had to be single-minded about nailing Cruzero. His mind had been made up months ago. He certainly wasn't going to let any feelings for a woman who had walked out on him get in the way of his ultimate goal. Play it cool, stay aloof, play a part. He still told himself that he was only using her to get Cruzero. That was why he allowed her to occupy only a small space in his life and not the whole of it. But he had to admit that she had gotten more of a grip of his emotions than he had anticipated.

He turned to her sleeping form. She lay exhausted by his lovemaking, alluring even in the soft peace of sleep. He acknowledged Sara had some kind of hold on him. Irritation made a small muscle in his jaw flex. He was determined to keep their relationship purely physical.

In the days and weeks that followed, Sara tried to avoid the issue of any more foreign assignments, as well as the thorny subject of the past and the equally thorny subject of Raphael Cruzero. Her emotional life with Alex was beginning to resemble a mine field. She trod carefully. They talked, they laughed, they spent time together, they made love, but the rift opened by the trip to Brazil had only narrowed, never entirely closed. Sara got the feeling Alex was waiting for something to happen, yet she couldn't put her finger on what it was. Was he testing her somehow? Sometimes she would catch his intent eyes on her, measuring her with one of his very Latin male looks. Was he figuring new ways and means to keep the woman of his choice under his control? Or was he only wondering if she was worth the trouble at all?

But he never put those thoughts into words. Despite his passionate nature and zest for life, he also had an innate Cuban reserve. It was driving Sara slowly stark raving mad, while Alex worked harder and later, becoming more and more obsessed by his job.

Chapter 9

The pictures Sara had taken in Brazil had impressed the editor from the travel magazine with her feel for the Latin American continent, for the whole Latin American ethos. He wanted to know if she was interested in another assignment and was waiting on the other end of the telephone for an answer. This time the trip was to Colombia. Now that she knew how Alex felt, apprehension mingled with her desire to go.

"We're doing a series on not-too-well-known places—places that are overlooked, underrated and still very good value for money. We were thinking of a photo essay on the coastal resort of Cartagena. It's far enough from Cali and Medellín to be safe for tourists. I know you once spent a lot of time in Colombia with your family. Like Brazil, you should have an instinctive feel for the place. We're sure that will come across in your work the way it did in Brazil.

"Colombia has developed a lot in the past fifteen years. I think you should get a good grip on the changes. This assignment won't come up for another couple of months, but I wanted to give you plenty of advance notice so you could get the time off from the newspaper. It's a week-long assignment. We want you to work the same way you did last time—just shoot the pictures that you yourself would want to see. Give us those and let us do the editing."

She knew the director of photography at the *Guardian* would give her a week off if she gave him enough notice. He was very flexible, but she had to make sure. "I'll have to check with the paper. I'll call you back."

As she put down the phone, Sara thought she would most likely call back and decline, but she hadn't wanted to say no outright. She wanted to give the matter some more thought.

Sara drifted into the newsroom and paused to talk to her friend Jessica. They indulged themselves in a cup of coffee and turned around when they over-heard the city editor talking to two reporters about a seizure of cocaine in a Miami warehouse.

The paper's hotshot young reporter, Jack Paterson, who had angled for a date with Sara on more than one occasion without success, drew her attention with a glint in his eyes. "Sara, here's something that might interest you."

She left Jessica and walked over where Jack stood with a leering smile. Tall and rangy with steel-blue eyes and a shock of black hair, he sank onto the edge of a desk next to her as the city editor said, "There's been a seizure of cocaine—six thousand pounds in a Miami warehouse.''

Another drug bust, she thought to herself. She looked at Jack Paterson, wondering why he thought that was significant.

The editor continued. ''But this one is unique. The cocaine was smuggled in cement fence posts.''

Again Jack Paterson's eyes danced with some inner knowledge yet to be sprung. She regarded him with only mild interest; another drug bust, even a sizable one, wasn't so unusual or exciting. She had covered too many of them by now and the novelty and fascination had worn off. Drug smugglers used hundreds of inventive ways to conceal the goods; fence posts weren't all that unusual. She wondered what Jack was getting at. He had something up his sleeve.

''They've arrested several men,'' he continued. ''One of them is a prominent Miami businessman.''

''Really,'' she said, showing polite interest.

''His name is Raphael Cruzero. Does that ring any bells?''

Her face blanched but she held on to her composure.

''I thought you might find that interesting,'' Jack said.

Now she knew why she had never accepted a date with him. She had never liked him, and now she had good reason not to. Everyone in the small enclave turned to look at Sara.

''Didn't you used to go out with him?'' Michelle Langley said. ''Of course! You were with him that night on the cruise. You went out with him before you and Alex became a couple. That night on the cruise he and Alex . . .''

Three pairs of inquiring eyes focused on Sara's face. Sara put down the paper coffee cup with a shaky hand. Others in the newsroom took note. Michelle wasn't the only one who had seen her with him on the cruise; several other people from the newsroom had been on the cruise, too.

''Are you sure it was Raphael Cruzero?'' Sara queried. ''Has he been arrested?''

''Early today,'' Jack confirmed. ''We have the names of the men arrested with him, but none of the others are from Miami.'' He showed her a list and she snatched it out of his hand, unable to believe it. Details of the arrest and the location of the warehouse jumped up at her. She was stunned speechless, even more so by his next words.

''Is this the first you heard of it?'' Jack queried with open speculation. ''Or can you give me some inside information, seeing how the man in your life is head of Centac? Centac made the arrest.''

Sara could see he was putting together a very juicy story in his mind. He had seen Alex waiting for her in the corridor outside the newsroom. He knew who Alex was, and Michelle Langley's comments had fired his interest more. Little escaped the grapevine of the newsroom.

''Did he tell you any details of the case for the record?''

She was being pumped for information and she knew it; the reporter was staring at her, measuring her reaction. Finding her words slowly, she answered, ''No, he never talks to me about his work and especially not about this case," she explained. Well, he had tried to warn her long ago, but she hadn't listened. Her mind had discounted his warning, and she had more or less forgotten about it. "I guess because I knew Raphael personally." She laughed softly at her own words. "You know how cops are about the media— always wary."

"Even when they're sleeping with one of them," someone inserted slyly behind her.

She turned around to see who it was, but couldn't detect who had made the rude remark. *Sleeping with one of them,* she thought bitterly. The same thing was running through all their minds.

"I'm as surprised by all this as anyone in the newsroom." She handed the sheet of paper back to the reporter, who still seemed to be waiting for some other kind of reaction from her regarding the accused.

"If it is true, and he is guilty, then I'm deeply saddened by it," she added to satisfy the questioning look in the eyes of the others. "I knew his family. We knew each other growing up." But that was only the half of it.

She turned and walked away toward the photography department with as much dignity as she could muster. But the news had come like a hard blow to her face. Not only because everything Alex had warned her about seemed to be happening, but also because Alex had kept her so completely in the dark, never mentioning a word. Even this morning at breakfast he had not said a word to her. He *had* to have known. She had found out about her friend secondhand from people in the newsroom, totally unprepared and taken by surprise with people gawping at her when she heard. That stung. It was not only remiss of Alex, it seemed a calculated maneuver. As if he wanted to wound her with the news in the worst way possible. To get back at her somehow for not believing him about Raphael. Resentment and anger over this rough treatment rose inside her. If it had been an isolated incident it would not have cut to the quick. But it was so characteristic of Alex lately. He never talked to her about his work, how his days went, never shared his thoughts or any of his inner feelings with her.

There was still a buzz of speculation among the reporters in the newsroom as to whether she was holding out on them. Her escape to the photography department freed her from the inquiring eyes but not from her own feelings of being mistreated. Then a few minutes later, to her dismay, the city editor sent her and Jack Paterson to the Miami warehouse where the cocaine concealed in fence posts had been seized.

When they arrived, police personnel were milling around, Alex standing nearby talking with two of his men. Sara froze inside at the sight of him. But she got on with her job, resentment at his treatment still fresh inside her. She wanted to get in and out as quickly as possible. Having taken all the pictures she could possibly use, she backed away. Alex was still talking, and she didn't know if he had seen her, nor did she care. She just wanted to get back to the newspaper.

With tension building inside her she was developing a headache. Wanting to relieve it before it got any worse, she searched her bag for aspirin. At last she found some in the bottom of her camera bag.

Pushing through the crush of journalists and officials, she hurried toward the nearest water fountain, tucked away in a corner beside a utility room. She swallowed the cool water and hoped to get relief soon. Her head was a throbbing drum.

She still felt shocked; she just couldn't believe that Raphael had actually been arrested. It didn't seem possible, that someone of his background could engage in drug trafficking, but it seemed to be true. She also felt betrayed. She had believed her old friend and he had been lying to her.

She straightened from the fountain. Someone loomed up behind her. When she turned around Alex stood there.

They kept their relationship strictly professional in public. Looking restlessly around to check that no one was within earshot, he spoke in a low voice. "Your friend is in big trouble, Sara."

At the moment she thought she hated him. Because he took such obvious pleasure in nailing her friend, she felt somehow he was getting back at her. Lifting her hand to blot the moisture from her lips, she watched his gaze follow the gesture.

"Now I know why you never discussed your work or told me about anything you were doing. Why do I have the feeling that you're not only serving the cause of justice but scoring some kind of personal vendetta—not only against Raphael but against me? You could have told me something about it when it was all tied up," she cried. "Do you know how I found out? Some reporter confronted me in the newsroom, trying to pump me for information."

"The ultimate responsibility for my unit rests with me. I can't talk about an investigation. You should know that by now." His smooth professionalism did nothing to reassure her, but only fanned the heat of her anger.

"You don't talk over anything with me—your work, your feelings, nothing. I have to find out in the newsroom what you're doing. Maybe someday I'll find out in the newsroom what you really feel for me. That is, if you have any feelings above your belt. Maybe I'm simply useful until you satisfy whatever it is you're after—revenge, lust, who knows."

"You're imagining things, Sara."

Her tone was low and tortured. "Am I, Alex? It's times like this when I don't think I know you at all, when I get the feeling I'm just someone you sleep with, someone you turn to in the middle of the night when the need arises."

"Come on." He closed his eyes with a look of forbearance. "Let's not get all dramatic about this." In spite of his obvious exasperation, she thought he looked uncomfortable.

"Thanks for telling me where I stand. Excuse me— I've got a deadline to meet."

As soon as she got back to the photography department she called the editor from the travel magazine. "I checked with the photography department," she told him. "I can get the time off. I want to take the assignment."

Chapter 10

Another big shock came at Raphael Cruzero's arraignment. Leo Coburn, Alex's brother-in-law, was defending him. Alex had already told Sara on more than one occasion that his brother-in-law was simply out for fat fees, not to serve the cause of justice. Precious few prosecutors could stand up to Coburn. He had the reputation of being some kind of legal Houdini.

News of his involvement in the case was met with despondency by everyone in the Narcotics Division, Sara heard. She knew Alex had already developed a jaundiced view of the whole proceedings. He recognized that his brother-in-law was a brilliant tactician, that he would employ any method—no matter how outrageous as long as it fell within the law—to get Cruzero off. The rest of the members of Alex's team felt equally uneasy when they discovered that Rapha-

el had switched attorneys at the last minute and hired
Leo Coburn to defend him.

The next painful experience was actually seeing her
old friend formally charged. The sight of him striding
in and out of the courtroom, handcuffed, his attorney at his side, was chilling; it sickened and saddened
her. Raphael was wearing a public mask, his face ex-
pressionless. His dark eyes stared stonily straight
ahead. For once his ebullient air was absent, his two-
thousand-watt smile missing. The judge had refused
bond, convinced Raphael would flee to Colombia.

Sara stood surrounded by a flock of reporters from
local newspapers and television stations. A galaxy of
camera flashes went off at split-second intervals, capturing Raphael's image on his way out of court. He
had made quite a name for himself in the Miami business community, so his alleged drug trafficking was
important local news. For a fleeting moment, Raphael glanced Sara's way. His eyes assessed her with the
same blankness as they viewed everything else, flick-
ing away again as if he did not recognize her.

"This is definitely not his finest hour," Jack Paterson said at her side.

Derogatory comments like that made Sara feel sick
inside. Blotting everything but her work from her
mind she got on with her job. But it was a painful,
disheartening task getting good still pictures of a former close friend of the family under such circumstances, to finally come to terms with the fact that
Raphael was what Alex said he was.

When she was finished, she saw Alex and a couple
of his men leaving the courtroom. The date was set for

the Raphael Cruzero trial, and with his brother-in-law defending him, Sara knew Alex was not going to be in the best of moods.

The next morning, immaculate as always in a well-cut suit that underscored his dark good looks, Alex stood at the counter with a cup of coffee, reading the morning headlines. The upcoming Cruzero trial hovered over him and Sara like a dark cloud. There was a closed-in reserve wrapped around him; he was autocratic and distant, yet she knew his mood could change in a flash to a passionate outburst; his temper was on a hair-trigger setting. A few moments ago he had been muttering about some development in the trial.

"You're becoming obsessed by this case," she said over the rim of her coffee cup.

Lifting his head he stared at her hard. "You think I like working my tail off to put one of these merchants of misery out of action and then watch it all be for nothing?"

"It's eating away at you. You've spoken two sentences this morning. Last night it was even worse."

"I keep wondering what kind of courtroom games Leo's going to get up to this time." He slammed the newspaper on the counter. Then he grinned at her sardonically. "You'd like to see Cruzero get off, wouldn't you?" The accusation was fired at her, bringing her sharply back.

Her gaze shot to his face with a guilty stab. "I never said that."

Lazy half-closed eyes assessed her unnervingly, as though he could see through to her backbone. "But you would like to see him get off. Admit it, Sara. You would like to see me proved wrong.''

''If a jury finds him innocent, I will be pleased in a way,'' she hedged.

Closing his eyes, he laughed softly to himself. *''In a way.* I like that. That's really something. You are a real piece of work, Sara. Do you mean in the way that means you are on his side, not mine!'' The Cuban temper erupted. Their eyes dueled in silence.

''I've never been completely convinced about his guilt—I don't deny that. I mean it would end your obsession to get him. I mean there might be some room left in your life for me. In that way it would please me, too,'' she retorted. She knew this conversation was entering dangerous ground. To avoid it, she started to walk past him, but his arm snaked out and he caught her.

''Wait a minute. Not so fast. Where are you going in such a hurry?'' His tone dropped to playful menace. He angled his head slightly to one side, smiling deceptively, amiably at her. The expression in his eyes said, *You're not going anywhere until I get what I want.*

''He's guilty as hell, but you still go on defending him. Why?''

''You're not right about everything.''

A dark eyebrow quirked in her direction. ''Okay, you're right about that. I'm not right about everything. But I have the feeling I'm right about this,'' he added on a lilting accented note.

The look in his eyes was challenging as he brought her inside the circle of his arms, until her warm body was close to his and the scent of her perfume hovered between them. She hadn't finished dressing yet; she was still wearing a blue silk robe with very little underneath.

"*Let's examine why* you feel this way."

"I already told you," she explained, putting her hands on his arms, trying to release herself. The smile stayed plastered on his face; he held up a finger, tapping her nose.

"It would make you very happy to be right and for me to be wrong. That's what's behind this continuing loyalty to your old friend." He drilled the meaning behind those words into her eyes. It was another sign of the wedge that was widening the gap between them.

"You would go against me, wouldn't you, Sara? To the bitter end you will defend this *friend* against me. Why?"

"I told you once before I never wanted to get in the middle of this. You were the one who dragged me into this, Alex. I resent it. Now you're becoming impossible to live with because it's all twisted up in your mind. Let me go."

"Remember what I told you. To get out of the middle you have to choose sides." His expression was serious, his tone explicit. "You are supposed to be on my side. You're either with me or against me."

"I don't have to choose sides. It's the jury's job to bring in a verdict. Not mine. You have a job to do and you did it. Now leave the rest up to the court and the jury. You're obsessed with this case, because there's nothing else in your life, Alex. We don't have a real relationship going for us. We only communicate on one level. It's not enough.''

He ignored her. ''Sara, I've got more than a year's work invested in this case,'' he reminded her.

''What about us?'' she pleaded softly. ''What about the time we've spent together? The time we've invested in each other? Isn't that worth something?'' She ran a hand through her hair, weary of the conversation. She turned away, the only evasion she could take, since his nearness still held her trapped against the side of the kitchen counter. But escape and evasion were never easily accomplished where Alex was concerned.

''We're not talking about Raphael. We're talking about you and me, Sara, about what and who comes first around here. I told you once before I don't take second place to anyone or anything.''

His hand caught the sash of the robe with a short pull, jerking her forward to get her attention back on his face. She dragged in her breath sharply, her hand clutching the two sides of the robe together. Alex moved closer.

''I'm a nice guy if you don't cross me. You wouldn't cross me, would you, Sara? How far would you carry this so-called loyalty to an old friend? Would you see Raphael behind my back? Would you play one of us off against the other? Don't even think of it.'' Alex forced the words out with autocratic grimness.

Her eyes widened on his face. His single-mindedness, which left no room for anything else except the goal he had in mind, showed her as nothing else could the ruthless streak in his personality. It also showed just how far the gap between them had widened. That he could have suspicions like this and take them seriously enough to confront her with them, only showed how far apart they were emotionally. It saddened her.

"I wouldn't go to see him behind your back," she murmured softly. "When I came here to live with you I stopped seeing him." Then thinking about his reference to Raphael, she added, "But if I did go see him there would be no risk involved, because I know he would never hurt me."

Alex's smile told her immediately what he thought of her reply. "You're underestimating him if you think that. You're underestimating me, too. Maybe you should be afraid of me, Sara, and what I might do if you did go to see him behind my back." He breathed the words against the side of her neck, pushing away the neckline of the silky robe as he kissed her collarbone.

His sensual assault stirred her blood. Her body quivered with an awakening response he aroused with predictable ease. She closed her eyes at the sensation, and her hand sank into his hair. Just as she fought off her own reluctance to respond to him, Alex seemed to be battling inner demons.

Their mutual reluctance was turning quickly into molten desire, but it was a workday, and they both knew it was getting close to the time they had to leave.

He lifted his head, hunger licking in his eyes. Not only did they clash over the outcome of the Raphael Cruzero trial, there was also the added prick of another free-lance photography assignment. He was too

proud to ask her to stay home again, but he couldn't
resist querying her about it, nor could he disguise the
resentment it evoked. He was reminding her that she
was going against his wishes.

"When are you leaving for Colombia?"

"In a few weeks, when the trial is on."

When the first day of the trial arrived and the defense's strategy unfolded, it turned out that Alex's
misgivings were more than justified. In the following
two weeks Sara watched Leo Coburn use every courtroom antic at his disposal to sway and confuse the
jury. Then he discredited the prosecution witnesses
and befuddled them by bombarding them with a blitz
of conflicting information.

Sara had been watching on and off from the press
gallery. Torn by her emotions, she was relieved when
the time came to leave for Colombia. The idea that
both she and Alex needed time apart from each other
was gaining strength in her mind. The tensions from
the trial and the upcoming trip hadn't diminished,
they had increased. If Raphael was found guilty she
didn't want to see it, and if he was found not guilty she
didn't want to have to face that accusing look in Alex's eyes if she displayed any signs of relief. She left
Miami International with the hope in her heart that
regardless of the verdict things would be settled by the
time she got back.

The morning Sara left for the airport the jury finally returned. After long deliberation they had not
been able to reach a unanimous decision. A federal
offense required a unanimous decision. The judge sent

them back to deliberate more, and several hours later they returned with a verdict of *not guilty*. Reporters made a beeline back to their newsrooms to write that the inexperienced prosecutor had never really stood much of a chance. There were precious few prosecutors that couldn't be eaten alive by a defense lawyer of Leo Coburn's caliber.

When she reached the airport in Cartagena, Sara dialed the newsroom from a pay phone. The reporter covering the trial told her the verdict. With her head bent, she replaced the receiver on the hook, flooded with mixed emotions.

In the taxi she closed her eyes, glad for the opportunity to get away, to lose herself for a while in her work. There was bitterness inside her when once again she thought of Alex's dedication to his job and his obsession to get Cruzero at the expense of his personal relationship with her. She also thought of the way she had become some kind of pawn. The feeling was growing stronger and stronger the longer she stayed with him.

It was Sunday, and the Cordera family had gathered for their customary afternoon together. Alex's gaze took in the sun-drenched patio, the graceful arches and tiled roof of his parents' home, the bougainvillea, the riot of color and lush foliage. The manicured lawns and underground sprinkler system testified to the fact that his family had come a long way since they arrived from Cuba with only the clothes on their backs. Various members of his family stood around talking. His nieces and nephews played in the large rectangular pool nearby that glowed like an aquamarine gemstone in the dazzling sunshine. He was alone; Sara was still in Cartagena.

His eyes narrowed on his brother-in-law as soon as he walked in and greeted everyone. Leo stopped to talk to Alex's father off on one side. Tall and lean, Leo wore his clothes with an air of studied ease, a man who selected everything with care—including juries, Alex reflected bitterly. In a few minutes Leo left his father and sauntered up to Alex. Uppermost in Alex's mind was the thought that Leo was the kind of guy who never knew when to quit. Even when he was ahead.

"Alex. How are things in the Narcotics Division? Will you be throwing any more new clients my way?" Droll amusement filled Leo's eyes. Alex knew he viewed the war on drugs as some kind of game. When Coburn was out of the courtroom he expected everyone involved in the court case to act as though the game was over and they were all pals again. He thought all was fair in love and war, especially when winning a case was involved.

Alex managed an amiable smile and maintained for the moment that innate dignity his Cuban heritage had dealt to him.

"Morale is high," Alex replied ironically. "It always makes us feel good when we work long and hard on a case and then we see it all go down the tubes. The stakeouts, the undercover work, the tedious attention to detail, the endless hours spent following up leads and checking out stories. Then some clown like you gets up in court and turns the justice system into a parody of what it's supposed to be. Does it give you a good feeling too, Leo, putting a man like Raphael Cruzero back on the streets, thwarting the cause of justice for the much better cause of lining your pockets?''

The pale blue ice of Leo's eyes crystallized imperceptibly. "You know I don't see it that way."

"I bet you don't," Alex remarked with a dark flash of sardonic amusement.

"The way I see it, the people accused of the most serious crimes are the ones most likely to be shunned by society and denied their rights. They're the very ones most in need of a strong defense, any defense within the law."

Alex's smile widened. Leo's high-minded justification of his courtroom antics seemed unassailable for a moment, so Alex let his gaze slide over the custom-made shirt Leo wore—Alex knew from Lourdis that he bought them by the dozens—over the impeccably tailored suit from some Palm Beach men's outfitter, to the Gucci loafers on his feet. He had heard also from Lourdis that Leo's office was furnished with an expensive computer system, an extensive library and some pieces of Chippendale straight from Sotheby's. It all served to punch holes in Leo's defense of himself.

"Especially when they can pay for it, Leo. That's what you're saying. The more money a man has the more justice he can get. Isn't that the way it works?" Alex wanted to see a little blood flow. The fact that Sara had gone off on the photography assignment only added fuel to his anger.

Leo leaned over with a false air of bonhomie. "Look, Alex. You shouldn't take the war on drugs so seriously. It's all a big game. Never lose sight of that and you'll be a happy man. Don't concern yourself with overall victory, just stay in the game. Why get all miserable about it?"

Alex's temper flashed. "Maybe if I were lining my pockets like you, I could play it as cool as you can. You competitive bastard, since when did you ever take losing gracefully?" Alex knew they were both highly competitive and neither of them was inclined to back down or bow out gracefully.

Leo looked casually around the patio. "Where's Sara today, Alex?" Having noticed the obvious, Leo wasted no time finding a needling gibe.

"She's on an assignment in Colombia." Alex waited, knowing his brother-in-law's enthusiasm for amateur psychology, in the courtroom as well as out of it.

"You know you can never trust a woman like Sara, Alex. When someone walks out on you once it must leave you with the uneasy feeling that one day she might do it again. My client Raphael Cruzero had a yen for Sara. But I guess you know that. If I were you I'd watch that situation very closely now that Raphael's been acquitted and may be thinking of heading back to Colombia."

"Leo, I wouldn't say anything else about Sara if I were you." Alex marveled that his brother-in-law was still standing there in one piece.

The deadly look in Alex's eyes warned Leo the fast-burning fuse of Alex's temper was reaching the flash point. But Leo was a guy who never knew when to quit. "You know what women like, Alex—a macho guy like you with a lot going for him below the belt. That's good enough to get you in the bedroom door, but what women really like is a guy with charm and polish and plenty of money. That's what you're up against with Raphael."

"Did I ever tell you that you're an easy guy to dislike?"

"Not in so many words. But I kind of get that feeling from time to time."

"But for my sister's sake, for my mother's sake, we have to *look* like we tolerate and respect each other. What I would really like to do is drag you to some isolated place and beat the living ... daylights out of you. But I'm not going to do that. Because I'm a reasonable guy and this is a family gathering."

He watched his brother-in-law jiggle the ice cubes around in his glass.

"You're a real tough guy, Alex, a real fiery Latino." Leo laughed dryly. With a glance sideways to see that his wife wasn't going to hear what he was saying, he finished his remarks. "You son of a bitch, I hope Cruzero gets Sara. You know something else? Nobody's forgotten the corruption charges brought against you and Centac. You'd better learn to like me because someday you may need me to defend you in court."

Alex closed his eyes, savoring the last remark. "No, Leo, I don't think so. Because only the guilty can afford your fat fees."

"Listen, I make *my* money within the law."

"I *live* within it. Don't you ever forget it," Alex reminded him through clenched teeth. Grabbing hold of Leo's lapels with the kind of sudden move that astounded people, he shoved Leo backward into the pool. The splash was enormous, testifying to the power behind the sudden thrust.

Shrieks of surprise from the family punctuated the air. Everyone leaped backward from the lapping water and a stunning silence suddenly prevailed. Then the children, who thought it was some kind of surprise game initiated by their uncles, screamed with delight, asking them to do it again. All eyes were on Leo as he spluttered to the surface, shaking his head like a cocker spaniel to get the water out of his eyes. A virulent stream of abuse hit the air, words a gentleman of charm and polish was never supposed to utter.

Alex smiled to himself as his brother-in-law waded laboriously toward the side of the pool. With everyone else standing well away, Alex walked over and offered a helpful hand. Leo glared at him and pulled himself out of the water using the ladder. His suit clung to his tall lean body and water squished from his Gucci loafers with a satisfying sound.

"You're going to lose Sara, you two-bit narc," he announced in a softly vindictive tone as he wiped water from his face with one hand.

"Remember, you win some, you lose some. It's all a 'big game.' Remember that and you'll be a happier man. You made a big splash, Leo." Alex smiled, knowing that was what Leo liked more than anything in life. Then the expression in Alex's eyes turned deadly again and he strode out the door, leaving his mother behind him wringing her hands and not knowing quite what to do, while his sister let loose a torrent of Spanish complaining to her father. The senior Mr. Cordera had watched the whole proceedings with unbiased interest, measuring his son and son-in-law, drawing his own conclusions.

People always said it was good to spend time with your family, Alex thought as he walked down the long winding drive toward his car. Intense anger still roared through his bloodstream, because whether he liked to admit it or not, Leo's verbal jabs had gotten to him. When he reached his car he didn't feel like climbing in, but he knew he had to go somewhere to cool down. What he really felt like doing was walking, just walking with no special place in mind. Loosening his necktie, he removed it, rolled it up and stuffed it into his jacket pocket. Then he unbuttoned his collar and slid into his car. His gaze skimmed the soaring royal palms that lined the drive. For a moment he stared unseeingly at the natural beauty that surrounded anyone living in Florida. He lit a cigarette.

Leo's remarks about Sara had really gotten to him, all right. He and his men had been exonerated from corruption charges, but his mind and heart still hadn't resolved his feelings for Sara. He knew that. He didn't like admitting it to himself, but nothing showed him better than a situation like this one how deeply she affected him.

Thinking about her, he drove to Little Havana and walked the streets for a while, then entered one of his favorite haunts, a Cuban restaurant that served black beans and rice.

After the sun went down he drove to a club on Miami Beach. Music played while flashing lights flickered over people's faces, his restless gaze swinging around as he leaned against the bar to watch but not really see anything. The atmosphere left him bored and restless. It wasn't what he wanted anymore. Yet he didn't want to admit to himself what he did want. After a while he made his way out of the crowded club onto the darkened street, found his car and drove home.

Inside the condo he tossed his jacket onto a chair. There were signs of Sara everywhere he looked and he tried to ignore them. A nightgown she had worn lay discarded on the foot of the bed when he walked into the bedroom. He balled it up and heaved it across the room into the open closet; he wanted no more reminders of her absence.

He hadn't figured on this. He resented the way she had made inroads into his mind. He was supposed to be standing back from any involvement, satisfying his physical desire but holding himself aloof. But incident after incident was dragging his true feelings out into the open. He was in danger of losing the battle with himself. And he didn't like himself for losing. He unbuttoned his shirt and shrugged out of it, tossing it aside. Sprawling his six-foot frame on the bed he studied the ceiling vacantly.

Returning from the week in Cartagena, relaxed, tanned and pleased with the way her work had gone, Sara walked slowly through the crowded concourse at Miami International Airport. She had forgotten to wear her wristwatch. When she lifted her gaze to check the clock on the wall, she saw Alex.

He was standing still, watching her intently. He dropped his cigarette to the ground as if he were considering something, then ground it out with his foot before he advanced toward her.

On the plane to and from Colombia Sara had done a lot of thinking about herself and Alex. The insidious thought that things would never work out between them was gaining momentum, causing her all kinds of mental anguish. With the gap between them widening, not narrowing, she caught herself thinking of moving back in with her sister. But now, seeing him waiting for her here made her heart clench with a spontaneous surge of joy. He had purposely come to welcome her back. Maybe this marked the beginning of a new era in their relationship, especially with the Cruzero trial behind them.

Rooted to the spot Sara watched him make his way through the jostling crowds. But the surge of joy rapidly faded when she saw the look in his eyes. Magnetically charged, it told her he was after something.

"Did you come here to meet me or are you here on official business?" she asked, suddenly wary, realizing he might be here for some other reason than to see her.

"I had to come here to talk with a customs official. When I heard you were coming in I thought I'd hang around and give you a ride home." The message behind the words was that he hadn't come all the way out here in the middle of a workday to meet her. She had just happened to fit in with his plans, so he'd decided to capitalize on the situation. Not for the first time, Sara had the inexplicable feeling that this was how it had been all along. They had gotten back together because she fit in with his plans. She felt like a fool for ever thinking otherwise.

"How are you?" he asked her.

"I'm . . . fine. How are you?"

His gaze darted to some distant point in space while he laughed softly. The word *fine* had special connotations for them both and she had used it deliberately to provoke him. The fact that he had come to see a customs official, not to meet her, still rankled.

"I think I'm fine. But it's been a long week, hasn't it?" he said with a quirk of his eyebrow.

"I thought the time passed very quickly," she retorted softly. "Oh, and you don't have to put yourself out on my account. I was thinking I might spend a few days with my sister. I can take a cab." She started walking away, thinking narrowly that she could easily make the stay with her sister indefinite, given the mood she was in.

His hand latched on to her arm, waylaying her. "You've been away for a week—forget about going to your sister. Why would you want to stay with your sister?" His steely regard impaled her. "I can drive you back to the condo. I've got enough time to spare."

"Because I think we need some time apart. It's not working out between us, it really isn't." She said the words underneath her breath, but that didn't lessen the sting behind them.

Alex's whole demeanor changed. She could see him regretting his thoughts fast. She watched him turning over this rebellion in his mind. People walked around them. Sara ignored them. Alex ignored them. They were locked in a world of their own making. They both knew things were coming to a head. Alex shot a sideways look at a woman passing next to him with two small children, then back to Sara.

"Let's get out of here. We can't talk here." His jaw was set into an adamant line. With his hard fingers closed around her arm he began propelling her out one of the exits of the terminal. Since he had her luggage she walked along acquiescently.

When they reached his car, Alex opened the door, took her gear and shoved it into the back seat. "Please get in, Sara," he commanded quietly.

The *please* surprised her. She sank into the seat and watched him walk around and get in the other side. When he had eased himself behind the wheel they both turned and looked at each other. The intimacy of the car closed around them, shutting out the brilliant day and passing sounds, encapsulating them in a tomb of glass and leather and chrome.

"Do you want to kiss me as much as I want to kiss you?" he murmured.

"No," she lied, expelling a shaky breath, turning her head away, when all she wanted to do was sink her hands into the warmth of his body, the thickness of his hair, to feel his mouth take firm possession of hers.

His expression hardened instantly. "Right." Moving away, he sprawled behind the steering wheel, his legs spread apart. He drummed hard fingers on the wheel, not letting her see the expression in his eyes. "So you think it's not working out between us."

"You hurt me, with your 'I can take you or leave you' attitude. I'm beginning to think we will only ever communicate on a sexual level. I'm really beginning to think it's hopeless."

"So you think *I hurt* you." He laughed softly to himself. He slipped his hands inside his jacket pocket and pulled out a cigarette. "These things are always two-sided," he announced enigmatically, lighting up.

"I don't recall doing anything to you without just cause," she retorted.

The lighter clicked shut. He shot her a fiery look. "I'll drive you to your sister's," he announced.

"Makes sense to me," she said glibly.

"It's nice to have this rapport going on between us all the time." The biting sarcasm behind his words belied the smile spreading across his face. The car engine sprang to life. Without looking at her again, Alex maneuvered the car into the passing traffic.

Sara could see emotions warring inside Alex. Suddenly without warning he turned the wheel sharply. Leaving the mainstream of traffic he swung into a side road and screeched to a halt at a deserted lot. The stop was so sudden, so violent, that she put out her hand to brace herself against the dashboard.

Hunching his shoulders, resting his arm across the back of the seat, Alex turned to her. His eyes narrowed on her face as if he wanted to eat her alive. "Sara, when you turn your back on me in any way— even for a trip a week long or a few days—it makes no difference, something inside me snaps. I can't be reasonable about it. I need you here with me." He jabbed his finger into space. "I need you to need me."

The words were fired out of nowhere, taking them both completely by surprise. She stared at him in stunned silence. It was the first time he had ever uttered some feelings that came from deep inside him, or let her in on what he was thinking. His words amazed her. But she was even more amazed that he had said them at all.

He moved quickly to reinforce what he'd said, cupping her face between his hands. "Do you understand what I'm saying to you? It isn't easy for me to ask you for anything but I'm asking you now. Don't turn your back on me again. I know that your work is important to you, Sara. From now on work around here," he concluded. "Will you do that for me, Sara?"

Her eyes searched his and she heard herself say "yes" but she was barely aware of her lips moving. She was so stunned by this sudden uncharacteristic display of inner feelings he usually preferred to keep hidden.

A smile transformed his face. "That surprises you."

"Yes," she murmured.

His eyes darkened with amusement. "I still want to kiss you. Are you going to go on playing hard to get?" he asked lazily.

"I don't think so." She smiled the words.

He smiled as he lowered his head. His lips were soft yet demanding, and she yielded to them when he took firm possession. When he lifted his head the warm gleam of his gaze perused her face. Satisfied, he put another question to her. "Do you still want me to drive you to your sister's?"

When Alex was like this she could refuse him nothing. "No, I don't think so," she heard herself say again. Her voice was a little breathless.

"I don't think so either." The gleam in his eyes deepened; his tone was a low intimate caress. His kiss was hot and passionate, searching and hungry.

When his car cruised to a stop in front of the condominium, he slammed out and walked around to her side, his hand shoving his tie inside his suit jacket. Without looking at her he opened the car door. Sara slid out. Bemused by his behavior, she retrieved her camera gear, while Alex reached into the trunk for her suitcase. She accompanied him to the entrance without a word.

At the door he looked down at her. His height overshadowed her. "I'll see you tonight."

That evening when Alex came in from work he devoured Sara with his eyes, then without preliminaries he tossed his jacket aside and drew her inside the hard circle of his arms. They began kissing hungrily. He breathed her name over and over between the heated initial foray of kisses. His restless hands caressed and molded her to him, kneading her flesh. Roughly tender, possessive, passionate, he aroused her rapidly, the meal she'd cooked for him forgotten. It wasn't food Alex had had on his mind all day long.

Later, after Sara had fallen asleep, Alex rose from the bed. Everything hadn't gone down the tubes when Cruzero was acquitted. For one thing, he had persuaded Sara to stay. For another, there was still a good chance of getting Cruzero. Narrowing his eyes, he lit a cigarette and inhaled deeply. A nagging voice inside his head said he was losing the battle with himself over Sara. His feelings for her kept coming out, and they had nothing to do with any personal desire to even an old score or any plan to nail Raphael Cruzero. The discovery disturbed him.

Chapter 11

Several weeks later, Alex stood in a dimly lit bar talking to an informant. The bar was crowded with people who didn't want to go home; it was Friday night.

"They're moving the cocaine in at night on a remote airstrip in Glades County."

Alex listened to the confidential informant with amusement. He had to hand it to Cruzero. The trial hadn't shaken him up or slowed down his operation. He had carried on dealing, probably right through the whole ordeal. With a renewal of his blind obsessive determination to get Cruzero at all costs, Alex remembered something someone in the department had pulled from an old saying. The wheels of justice moved slowly but when they rolled they grind you into powder. Alex intended to turn Raphael and his whole operation into powder as fine as the white powder he was responsible for distributing on the streets. But there were thirty or forty airstrips scattered around Glades County. He had to figure which ones to target.

The informant, who had been a drug runner himself once for the Cali cartel, said that he knew most of the airstrips. Both men hunched over the bar, surrounded by earsplitting music, and speculated on which ones were most likely.

Later in the week, working with the Glades County police force, Centac staked out several. This time, for a change, luck was with them. In the early hours of a Sunday morning they intercepted a two-thousand-kilo load. By sunrise they had arrested half a dozen people—pilot, ground crew, the man who owned the land—and taken them into custody.

That evening Alex sat in his office reflecting. Now he not only had the woman Raphael wanted, but he also had his latest shipment of cocaine. It had been no piggyback venture, where a shipment was to be delivered to several dealers. The DEA informant said that to the best of his knowledge the cocaine was all Cruzero's. The seizure, coming in the wake of an expensive trial, had to have put a sizable hole in even Raphael's resources. Even though he had been acquitted the trial had left a blight on his reputation in the Miami business community. Alex speculated with a wry smile that Raphael wasn't feeling in the best of moods. In fact, Alex bet that Raphael was hopping mad. When a man was mad, he often made king-size mistakes. Raphael was the kind of guy who would strike back hard where it would hurt most. He knew he wanted Sara.

Time crept by slowly on a stakeout, especially when you had no one with you to talk to. Concealed from the road by a screen of trees, Alex sat inside a parked car, watching the window of the second-floor apartment he and Sara shared. A radio receiver was propped up on the dashboard. He had planted a wiretap on the telephone in the condo, so he could listen in on all the phone calls Sara received or made.

His suspicion that Raphael would try to contact her had grown into a certainty in his mind. How Sara would react to any overtures, he wasn't sure. Doubts about how she felt about Raphael still lingered in his mind. He didn't trust her where Raphael was concerned, he never had. But he didn't think she would go with him willingly; he thought Raphael would have to use force if he wanted to take her.

The telephone in the condo rang twice before Sara picked it up. Her voice flowed over the radio receiver into the car, soft with a slight huskiness that always turned Alex on. Instantly alert, he listened for a few moments, then tuned out. It was only one of her friends from the newspaper—female chat didn't interest him. Looking out the window of the car, he took in the moonlit star-spangled sky, listened to the edges of palm fronds rustle softly in the night breeze. He lit a cigarette, then let his gaze wander down the dark street, watching for vehicles and people going in and out of the condominium block. He still wasn't familiar with all the residents' cars, but he knew most of them.

About an hour after Sara had spoken to Jessica, the phone rang again. She had just emerged from the shower and was giving herself a manicure. She walked over and picked up the phone.

"Sara, I've been trying to reach you for the past half hour." Her sister's voice rolled out of the receiver.

"Hi. Sorry—I was on the phone with one of the women from the newsroom and then in the shower. Maybe I didn't hear the phone when it rang."

"How are you? What are you doing?"

"Nothing much, just mooching around."

"Where's Alex?"

"Working, of course. Where else!" Sara laughed softly but she couldn't disguise the slightly bitter edge in her tone. She didn't like the way it sounded but it was there, a telltale sign for the whole world to pick up on. Her sister picked up on it immediately.

"How have things been since you got back from Colombia?" Her sister knew that since they had gotten back together everything had not gone as smoothly as Sara had hoped. But since Alex had opened up and told her how he felt, Sara had given her word and intended to stay no matter what happened. She wouldn't turn her back on him again.

"We're still sort of living side by side but each doing our own thing," she murmured. "We communicate on only one level," she added quietly.

The gap between them still remained. Except for that one revealing glimpse of himself on the way home from the airport, Alex had gone straight back to his former way of doing things. It was as if the devastating charm and intimacy had been turned on with some specific purpose in mind. Having achieved it, he went back to working twelve- and fourteen-hour days. But she knew in her heart that she loved him. That was why she was here. That was what counted.

But there had been another turn of events that had changed the whole complexion of things recently and really left her reeling. Running a hand through her hair, she thought she could tell her sister. If she didn't tell someone close to her, she was going to explode.

"So the status quo is that we're totally hooked on each other, but I can never shake the feeling that I'm here on some kind of trial basis or that I simply fit in with his plans. Our modus vivendi is trying not to step on each other's sensitive spots. Silly, isn't it? But that's the way I feel and I can't shake the idea. It keeps coming back to me."

"You're imagining things." Her sister laughed. "What kind of trial basis could there be—you only have to see how he looks at you to know that you're not there on any kind of trial basis."

"Maybe you're right." Sara laughed with relief. Her younger sister was no slouch when it came to sizing up a situation. "But I think it's more complicated than that. And it's getting more complicated all the time," she added on a rueful sigh.

"What do you mean?"

"I think I'm pregnant," Sara finally confessed in a low voice.

"But that's wonderful! What did Alex say?"

"I haven't told him."

"Why ever not? You love him, don't you?" her sister rushed on.

"Oh, I love him all right. Sometimes I love him so much it hurts," she retorted in a low voice.

"Then why haven't you told him?"

"Because of what happened seven years ago, I'm not sure how he's going to react. I'm not sure if he's going to feel trapped, angry, pleased—who knows? Your guess is as good as mine. These days I never know what's going on in Alex's mind. He rarely tells me anything. But I will tell him eventually. I've just been waiting to make sure." She was positive; she was dragging her feet and she knew it.

"You have to tell him. It's his right to know. The sooner you tell him the better...."

Alex sat frozen in silence in the front seat of the car. He stubbed out the cigarette with a mixture of emotions flooding him—proud elation mingled with anger, surprise and dismay. *Sometimes I love him so much it hurts. I think I'm pregnant. I'm not sure how he's going to react.* Sara's words bounced around in his head. They tugged at his deepest feelings for the woman he had always wanted, wrenching them to the surface.

Sara kept on talking to her sister about what a baby would mean, prolonging the pleasure of talking about the event, when the doorbell interrupted their conversation.

"I'll be right back," she murmured into the receiver. "Don't go away." An "okay" floated back to her followed by a "don't keep me holding on too long." With those words spurring her on, Sara put down the receiver on the table and hastened to the door, her long robe swishing around her legs.

"Who is it?" she queried, poised in front of the door, one hand resting on the knob. A voice throbbed through the paneled door that it was the repairman checking out all the air-conditioning units in the block of condos. "They would come now," she muttered to herself.

Unlocking the door in a hurry, with her sister waiting on the telephone and their conversation uppermost in her mind, she didn't bother with the safety chain.

Two dark-haired Hispanic men in work clothes confronted her. One, stocky and powerfully built, smiled ingratiatingly. His wide smile revealed a gold-capped tooth. The other man was taller and leaner.

She smiled pleasantly back. "Our air-conditioning unit is okay. It's running per—"

The two lunged forward suddenly. The stocky man grabbed her, swinging her around. The other man slammed the door shut with reverberating force. A large hand clamped over her mouth. Her eyes widened wild with shock. For a moment, she was paralyzed with fear.

Coming back to life, Sara began the struggle to break free. But she was caught in a viselike grip, pitted against bull-like strength and dragged into the center of the room. Struggling to break the hold, she bit down sharply on the thick fingers that covered her mouth and her leg lashed out, kicking a table, sending a lamp crashing to the floor. Suddenly her mouth was free and a long piercing scream filled the air. She was dimly aware it was her own. The man swore violently.

Instantly the hand clamped back down onto her mouth, this time harder, threatening to suffocate her. Rocking her against his hard body, the man bound her to him again. The second man loomed in front of her stricken eyes. She got out another piercing cry just as he taped her mouth. The tape choked off strangled pleas to let her go. Only muted cries of desperation surfaced now. The phone lay off the hook with her sister calling frantically to her. The second man slammed the receiver back down into the cradle.

Sara watched her lifeline with her sister cut in two. Everything was happening so fast. A chaotic jumble of panic and terror gripped her. There was no thought in her mind; instinctive primitive reactions and blind panic had taken hold. She fought and twisted and writhed, using up precious energy. She was pinioned against the swarthy stocky man who held her captive; he laughed in her face, showing his gold-filled teeth, and whispered obscenities in her ear. Her fevered vision saw the second man readying a syringe. With her mouth taped and her hands locked behind her she fought with every ounce of strength she had left, screaming silently in her mind: *No! No! No!* But her rising desperation came out only in pitiful, incoherent sounds against the tape covering her mouth. Using her leg, the only weapon she had left, she made

one last stab at thwarting them. Kicking as high as she
could, she went for the man's arm. A blow to his el-
bow knocked the syringe out of his hands as he approached. He swore at her again and something
exploded against the side of her face. Sara blacked
out.

"Estás loco." The stocky man shouted at the other
in Spanish that Raphael would kill them if she was
hurt.

Alex heard the skirmish and Sara's piercing screams
over the radio receiver in the car. Charging out of the
car, he sprinted at full speed toward the condo, drawing the gun from the holster underneath his jacket. He
bypassed the ground-floor elevators and raced up the
stairs. When he reached the second-floor landing Alex
flattened himself against the wall. Inching forward he
shot a quick glance through the narrow glass pane in
the stairwell door. All he saw was the empty corridor
of the second floor.

To the best of his knowledge the men were still inside the condo. His training, cool professionalism and
instinctive reactions were in full play, but for a fleeting moment he realized all that he wanted was in the
balance. If Raphael had managed to kidnap Sara to
Colombia— In a foreign country, tied to Raphael
without papers or any resources of her own, Sara
could disappear forever without a trace. He could lose
Sara forever this time, and his child, too. His desire to
get Cruzero had insulated his mind against the very
real risks involved, blinded him to the consequences.
Or had it been his refusal to face up to the depths of

his emotions regarding Sara? Whatever way he looked at it, he thought, closing his eyes at the painful knowledge, he had been a damned fool. Why had he been so blind? Everything he'd ever wanted had been there at his fingertips; all he'd had to do was reach out and take it. Now it was in danger of being taken from him. All that was male and protective rose up inside him.

Bringing the radio to his mouth he called in his position, and announced that some men were attempting to abduct a female. With one eye still on the door to the condo, he added that he was on his own and needed backup.

Suddenly the door to the condo opened and two men emerged. Alex dropped to the floor, flattening himself back against the wall, using his peripheral vision. He saw one of them half dragging, half carrying Sara. Her cascading hair obscured part of her face. Tape covered her mouth. Barefoot and clothed only in a houserobe she looked dazed.

Bursting through the stairwell door, he trained his gun on them both with two hands and shouted, "Police! Freeze!"

The taller man went for a gun. With split-second timing Alex fired twice. The impact of the bullets knocked the man backward, and he stumbled, firing wide of his intended victim. Alex's gun swung back to the man holding Sara. He, too, pulled a gun. Using Sara as a human shield he held it to her temple, backing away at the same time.

Coming around, Sara focused hazily, locked in the man's paralyzing grip. The realization of what was happening to her widened her eyes with fear. Alex kept on coming at him like a Mack truck, forcing the man backward down the corridor. The swarthy man, built like a bull, kept backing away with one eye on him, lurching down the corridor with Sara stumbling along with him, obviously terrified.

There was another stairwell at the other end of the hall. The man darted a glance toward it. Alex knew that since he had forced him past the elevator the man was headed for those stairs—the only avenue of escape he had left. He knew the Colombian wanted to get him off his back; he was waiting for the other man to shoot him. Suddenly the gun moved away from Sara's temple and fired. Alex dived into an open doorway as two shots exploded past him into the wall.

Tears were rolling down Sara's pale cheeks. The man continued to drag her away, and she staggered barefoot down the corridor with him. The killer instinct so integral to his personality surged inside Alex. Adrenaline pumped into his veins. His gaze locked onto the man waiting to get a clear shot at his head, as that man replaced the gun to Sara's temple. Alex waited for that next all-important movement—the moment the man turned his head again, the moment he knew was coming.

The man turned. In a split second reaction Alex fired. Deadly accurate bullets hit their target. The man wore a stunned expression. He fell back against the wall, his eyes wide open. His hold on Sara relaxed.

Alex immediately swung his gun back to the first man, who was struggling to his feet. Alex lunged toward him, dragged him up against the wall and shouted orders in his ears. He shoved the man's head against the wall with one hand, so that his face was pressed to the side and locked into that position, then his free hand reached for the handcuffs on his belt.

Like a wounded animal Sara scrambled on her hands and knees out of the way to the opposite side of the corridor, where she cowered against the wall. Everything had happened in less than three minutes, Alex guessed. Shoot-outs always happened with mind-boggling speed. With his gaze still pinned on both men, he moved back to where he'd dropped the police radio by the stairwell door.

Sara stood in a doorway, white-faced and shaken. Her trembling hands finally succeeded in pulling the tape from her mouth.

Alex looked at her. "Sara, go inside the apartment," he ordered abruptly. There was just a hint of tenderness in his voice.

The voice of the dispatcher filled the air. Backup was on the way—two squad cars that had been patrolling a nearby neighborhood. Alex replied to the dispatcher that the situation was under control. He asked for the medics.

Sara inched her way along the wall, stumbling past him on shaky legs. Her gaze was still riveted to the man with the head wound, who had slumped to the floor, as if she feared he would rise and attack her again. Blood oozed from his head, forming a dark wine-colored pool on the soft green carpet. For a moment she stared at the blood, fascinated. Then, suddenly covering her mouth with her hand she rushed inside the condo to the bathroom.

She leaned over the basin and splashed her face with cold water, sobbing quietly. She dried her shaking hands and stared at herself in the mirror; her silver-gray eyes were bright with shock.

When she emerged a few moments later, white-faced but feeling steadier, Alex's backup had arrived. Uniformed cops had taken the two men into custody. The other occupants of the building were crowded into both ends of the corridor, pushing and shoving to see what was going on, chaos threatening. Two of the uniformed policemen herded them back, ordering them to leave space for police personnel and arriving medics. Leaning against the doorframe, Sara stared at the activity. Voices droned in the background. Everything had happened so fast, but there had been no sense of time. From the time the two men rushed at her in the condo to the end of the shoot-out in the hallway, it had been like some kind of suspended animation, only with everything still moving—a paradox, but that was the only way she could describe it. The action had been so highly charged, had such blinding impact, like a series of continuous hard blows to the face, yet in a kind of spaced-out vacuum. Now everything had been transformed again and another sort of chaotic activity surrounded her. Dazed, she heard everything, she saw it all, but it was as if she were miles away from it; she was not part of it.

She wanted to go to Alex. She wanted him to hold her in his arms; she wanted to bury her face in the curve of his neck, to feel the solid reassuring warmth of him, to feel the steady pounding of his heart. But he stood talking to one of the uniformed officers. The other two uniformed policemen stood nearby, a barrier between the wounded men and the curious tenants crowding into the hall.

Sara's numbed mind began to function. Who were those thugs? What had they wanted with her? Where had they been going to take her? Her gaze slid back to Alex for the answers. With a remote look of wonder in her eyes she contemplated him, as if seeing him for the first time. She had never observed him in a life-threatening situation before, so she had not appreciated fully just how good he was at his job. The decisive split-second reactions, the deadly aim and the equally deadly fixed stare as he moved down the hallway, forcing the man relentlessly backward—it had all been stunning to behold. She would never forget the look in his eyes for as long as she lived. She knew it was part of his training, but she was still in awe of what she had seen.

Love welled up inside her, along with fervent gratitude that he had happened to be near the condo when all this took place. It seemed like some kind of miracle.

She watched him lift the police radio to say something. His dark head ducked momentarily and her eyes rested on his broad-shouldered back. The powerful, leanly muscled frame, the suit he wore, were achingly familiar to her, but she had the unnerving sensation she didn't know the man inside them at all. She had never really gotten to know the man, only that impressive charismatic facade he showed to all the world. The man at his side said something that made him turn in the other direction. Elevator doors slid open and four medics hurried through, two with a stretcher, the other two with life-support systems. They clustered around the more seriously wounded man.

Almost simultaneously another man arrived, pushing through the stairwell door. Sara instantly recognized Mike Garcia. He and Alex conversed in low tones. Sara watched Alex; it was as if she couldn't take her eyes off him. He had just shot two men, possibly mortally wounded one, yet his outward demeanor showed few signs of it. She watched him reach inside his jacket for a cigarette.

How lucky she had been, she thought. He must have been on his way home. How else could he have gotten there so fast? But hadn't he told her he was working the night shift? She thought she remembered him saying not to wait up for him because he wouldn't be back until the early hours of the morning. The strange remote sensation had left her feeling light-headed and confused. It was hard to think straight, she thought. What else could she expect after what she had just been through? Closing her eyes for a moment and leaning back against the wall, she clutched the sides of the neckline of her silk robe.

At precisely that moment Alex's head turned in her direction. Now that the wounded men were being taken care of and the situation was firmly under control he could leave it for a few moments. He said something to Mike Garcia before leaving him.

"It was a good thing you set up that wiretap, Alex, that's all I can say."

Sara thought those were Garcia's words, but for the moment, in her dazed state, she didn't attach any significance to them. Other questions were crowding into her mind. She opened her eyes.

Alex stood over her, his eyes filled with concern. "How are you feeling, Sara?"

"I was never so terrified in my life," she whispered.

"Sara…" He started to say something and lifted his hand to the side of her face. She winced when he touched the tender spot from the hard blow to her face. His eyes burned with the knowledge she had been hurt. He pulled the sash on her silk kimono tighter, then drew the sides of its neckline closer together. There was an aching tenderness in his movements that filled her eyes with tears.

"Hey, you should go and put some clothes on." He ran his hands down the silky material, locking them on her waist. Lowering his head, he murmured against her temple, "Those guys over there will be getting excited." He rested his head against her forehead. She watched him close his eyes. His hands suddenly clamped spasmodically on her waist, possessively, drawing her in to him with the air of a man who had come close to losing something he realized he could never replace.

"Are you going to be all right when I leave here, Sara? I have to go down to my office in a little while. When I'm through there I have to get back to the hospital. I want to question the one who's in good enough shape to talk." He indicated the hallway with a slight nod of his head. She read a silent apology in his eyes when he surveyed her face.

"You look dazed, shell-shocked. Maybe I should call your sister to come and stay with you. Or do you want me to get you a drink?"

She shook her head. "Just tell me who they were. What did they want? They didn't try to steal anything." She frowned. "Why did they want me?"

"You sure you don't want something to drink?"

She shook her head, still waiting for an answer. His demeanor changed, quickening.

"They're Raphael's men, Sara. I would stake my life on it. Trained kidnappers, hit men." His eyes burned the seriousness of his words into her flesh. "If they had succeeded, in getting you out of the country... Sara, I almost lost you. I don't want to think about it." The words emanated from him with a rough tenderness while his hands tightened on her waist again. She leaned against him, closing her eyes; this time she didn't question what he said about Raphael; she accepted it. She breathed in his clean male scent, clinging to him for support and comfort. But thoughts kept parading into her mind.

"How did you manage to get here so fast, Alex? Your timing was close to miraculous. If you had gotten here five minutes later, I would have been gone."

"It's not important. I got here in time—that's what counts."

Something about his reply bothered her. Lifting her head, she leaned back in his arms. "Did I hear Mike Garcia say something about a phone tap?"

"I was out in the street, sitting waiting in a car, listening to your telephone conversation on a radio receiver."

"Waiting?" Confusion clouded her eyes.

"Waiting for Cruzero to make a move," he stated with a look in his eyes that said he wanted very much to talk to her about *that* telephone conversation. If her mind had not been busy trying to sort out something disturbing, she would have appreciated the look in his eyes. Something about this situation was wrong. She was desperately trying to put her finger on what it was.

"You mean all along...you knew something like this was going to happen?"

He reached out to touch her neck, to bring her closer to him again. She could see an intense expression entering his eyes. It was a look that said he knew his next words were very important. This was one of those pivotal moments in a relationship that could go either way. He had the look of a man who was going to get it to work for him, not against him.

"I figured something like this was going to happen sooner or later, Ṣara."

"Sooner or later. What do you mean? When did you start thinking like that?" Suddenly her mind zeroed in on what it was that was so disturbing. "Was this some kind of entrapment situation?" she asked slowly. "Is that what you're saying?"

Chapter 12

She waited, but he didn't deny it or confirm it. He had the look of a man weighing something in his mind and deciding whether or not to tell her.

"Did you set this up?" she persisted with an uneasy feeling still stirring inside her.

"I figured on something like this happening, Sara. I made it work for me. I didn't set it up." His hands clasped her shoulders.

Her eyes widened imperceptibly as the thrust of his meaning struck home. She took two unsteady steps back from him. She wanted to distance herself from all that formidable macho charm so that she could think straight. When he was was holding her, he swayed her in whatever direction he wanted her to go.

"Made it work for you..." she ventured tonelessly. "Did making it *work* for you include using me as bait?" she finished on a scornful note. His expression altered. "Is that why you wanted me to move in here with you?"

"Sara," he said in low vibrant tones, not wanting the others to hear. "You wanted me. I wanted you. That's why you're here with me."

"To keep you satisfied while you get things to *work* out for you. Why not provide yourself with a little entertainment while you got the job done!"

Alex's eyes darkened for a moment to velvet intensity, then he looked restlessly over his shoulder. The line of his mouth thinned. Mike Garcia was only a few feet away waiting, listening, watching. Two of the uniformed cops still hovered nearby as the medics maneuvered stretchers out of the corridor, taking the wounded men down in the elevator. Curious people were still clustered at both ends of the hallway watching.

Alex angled his head slightly downward, avoiding her eyes, and his tone dropped to intimacy. "Sara... this is not the time or the place." He packed a wealth of meaning into the way he spoke her name, but Sara wasn't receptive. She wasn't even listening. When he lifted his gaze, she was without mercy, and just as ruthless with his feelings as he had been with hers.

"How far did all this go? Was getting me to love you part of getting things to *work* for you, Alex? Was saying you had to see me part of getting things to *work* for you?" She softly jeered at him but her eyes filled with tears, and her lower lip trembled with the effort it was costing her to put these strong emotions into words.

For a fleeting moment his eyes were filled with something akin to pain. He looked over his shoulder. "We'll talk this over when we're alone."

"No," she commanded mutinously. "We'll talk this over now. Here. This minute. If you've got nothing to be ashamed of, you can tell me here and now."

Her strident tone achieved the direct opposite of what she wanted. Everything about Alex turned instantly steely. Everything that was macho in him rose up. He held up a hand in a gesturing of warning. No woman talked to him like that, even when she had just cause.

"We'll talk about this later, when we're alone. Do you hear what I'm saying?"

His arrogance fell on deaf ears. "Why can't you give me any answers now, here in front of your men? If what they think is more important to you than what I'm feeling right now, then we don't really have anything to talk about, do we?"

His hand reached out to touch her but Sara was quivering with rage, her eyes filled with fury. "And don't touch me," she snapped.

When she turned her back on him, she sensed the male frustration pulsating from him. The highly trained professional so cool in the line of fire, spurned by the woman he wanted, was doing one of his famous slow burns. But it gave her no pleasure and she had no desire to gloat.

Still shaky and disoriented but no longer blind to what had been going on for the past few months, she wandered into the bedroom. Her senses were still reeling from all that had happened in one evening but only one idea dominated her thoughts. She was not going to stay with him a minute longer. Looking down at the robe she was wearing, she quickly untied the sash and took it off.

When Sara emerged fully dressed from the bedroom into the living room, Alex was still talking to Mike Garcia, barring the entrance to the condo. Most of the people were drifting away now that the wounded men had been removed. Alex turned to look at her. His eyes were molten pools of macho reticence. When she told him she was leaving and that she would come back later for the rest of her things, the two men in uniform shot furtive glances their way, suspecting that something heavy was going on between Lieutenant Cordera and the young blond-haired woman. But they quickly looked away again with an expression that said it was none of their business. Mike Garcia shot a sidelong look at his boss that assessed the situation sharply. Sara watched Alex ignore it.

"Let me drive you to your sister's. You're in no condition to drive." He ground out the words underneath his breath.

"I'm fine," she murmured. "I'm just fine."

Alex's sensual mouth tightened. He stared at a point over her head, reining in his temper. Garcia discreetly walked away.

"All right, Sara. If this is the way you want it, I won't try to stop you."

"Thanks. By the way, the next time you want to use me, you'd better ask first. I liked to be asked." She smiled coldly at him. His eyes burned into her face. Icy professionalism shot back at her.

"We need you down at the division tomorrow to give us a formal statement."

"I'll be there."

That night it was a long time before Sara fell asleep. She couldn't believe what had happened or how blind she had been to what had so obviously been going on all along. The months since she had returned to Miami kept going through her mind. Certain events stood out so glaringly, she wondered how she had failed to see the obvious. The way Alex had walked into her life, the look in his eyes that night she was with Raphael at the Polo Lounge. She should have been warned then; his parting look had been an indication that maybe it had been a mistake to come back onto his turf. Then there had been the night outside the Country and Western Tavern when she had had a glimpse of his true feelings, the unleashed anger that had been brewing for seven years. He wanted to exact some kind of retribution. That had been another sign she had ignored, thinking that once his anger was out in the open it was spent. But she had been wrong again. The apology telling her he was out of line had only been a ploy to get to see her again. Was that when it started? Was that when he had decided to use her while he got things to work for him?

Her mind skipped to other times, other places, other things Alex had said and done. There was the night of the cruise, the ugly explosion of violence between the two men. Then there was the time he had come to see her, when he told her Raphael had set him up, when he had told her she had to choose sides and get out of the middle. It had all been leading up to getting her back—to satisfy his male ego, to fulfill his need to get even and his desire to get Cruzero. It was all woven together so neatly. She remembered his words at the time that had so deeply affected her, the way he had so easily lured her, manipulated her completely back into his life.

I have to see you, again, he'd said. Of course he had to see her. Every move he made had been leading up to it. It was all part of getting things to *work* for him. She turned her face into the pillow. Oh God, why hadn't she seen it coming? Was she always destined to make a complete fool of herself where Alex was concerned? The afternoon at his parents' house, his sister had warned her about his being obsessed with his work, but she had ignored the warning. His wanting her to move back in with him, telling her he wasn't satisfied, using her desire for him—with the wisdom of hindsight it was all so obvious now. The way he'd exploded when she left the country, telling her it was because of the other time she left him, that something snapped when she turned her back on him. It was laughable now. The real reason he hadn't wanted her to go was that it didn't fit in with his plans.

Unable to sleep, Sara finally rose to her feet and wandered to the window. She stood gazing out, her head pressed against the draperies, her eyes staring unseeingly into the balmy night. What was she going to do now? What on earth was she going to do now? she asked herself. She was pregnant with his child and he didn't love her. Just like seven years ago. He never

had loved her. For all she knew he wouldn't know love
if it hit him in the face.

The next day Sara walked into the Narcotics Division feeling wounded and battered.

Dark, imposing and macho, looking anything but
repentant, Alex wasn't showing any remorse in front
of his colleagues. He stood waiting, his eyes burning
holes into her when she walked in. Mike Garcia stood
nearby. Both men seemed to be waiting for someone
else.

She shot Alex a questioning look that didn't conceal the deep resentment that flowed in hot streams
inside her when she regarded him.

"We're waiting for the stenographer," he announced, seeing the look in her eyes and measuring it.
She barely looked his way again. It had been a long
night; she had lain awake for many hours until she finally fell asleep. She was not in the best of moods.

"I came here to give a formal statement. That's the
only reason I'm here," she announced pointedly.

"I'm glad you could make it, Sara," he said dryly.
"It all helps if you want us to put these guys away.
Know what I mean?" His sharp-edged humor was
firmly in place as he indicated a chair near a table with
a casual gesture of his hand. She turned around and
looked at it for a long moment as if she was still deciding on whether to go or stay, then sank slowly into
the seat with her eyes on his face.

The evocative searing sound of the friction of ny-
lon-clad thighs filled the silence in the office as she
crossed her long legs provocatively. Alex's gaze fol-

"I think I know you now. I know one thing for sure, you haven't stopped loving me, Sara. I only have to touch you to know that."

The way he delivered that observation, the arrogant assurance behind it, only inflamed her sense of outrage. "Maybe not. Give me some time to work on it," she finished on a hollow note.

The elevator doors opened at last and she stepped inside. Facing him, frozen-faced, she watched the doors swish closed and heard something that sounded like a fist pounding against the wall as the elevator began its swift descent. Alex could swear just as fluently in both Spanish and English; she heard both echoing down the elevator shaft.

Torment and anger had been visible in his face and eyes but she had hardened her heart to it. *Now* he wanted to talk. What about all those weeks and months together when they could have talked about so many things, she thought resentfully. He'd never told her what he was thinking, never told her what he was feeling, there were times when he had barely talked at all. Now she was the one who didn't feel like talking. She wanted to see him squirm, she wanted to cause him torment, she wanted to watch him stew in his own juice. She lifted a shaky hand to her face, covering it.

His words came back to her: *you are carrying my child.* In the early stages of pregnancy her hormones were in a state of flux; she was highly emotional. Hardening her heart toward Alex was never easy even at the best of times when her confidence was running high. Now it was at an all-time low. She felt demolished by events. Still she knew she had to be tough, in order to protect herself.

By the time she got to the ground floor she was fighting back tears. She walked quickly to the entrance, practically racing to get to her car before she lost control of her composure. Colliding with someone on her way out, she excused herself in a taut emotionally charged voice and eventually reached the parking lot. Inside her car, she locked her hands together on the steering wheel, closed her eyes and rested her face against the backs of her hands, trying to regain a sense of calm. She had a luncheon engagement and she didn't want to turn up with suspiciously red eyes.

After Sara left the division, Alex sat in his office experiencing his bittersweet victory over Raphael. With testimony from the Colombian in custody who had survived the shoot-out and from the men arrested in the cocaine seizure in Glades County, the division thought they had an open-and-shut case this time. Not even a legal Houdini like Leo Coburn would get Cruzero off this time.

But what price had Alex paid for revenge? The one woman he had ever truly loved, the woman he wanted more than any other, wouldn't let him near her. He put a weary hand to his eyes, then swung around in the desk chair and rose out of it in one fluid motion. He adjusted his tie and shrugged into his jacket, then picked up some keys from his desk. His eyes were dark with smoldering determination. He had been cooling his heels long enough. He made up his mind that sooner or later he was going to catch her alone. They would have their talk.

But that evening when Alex tried to call Sara, her sister told him she didn't want to talk to him and please not to call again, his calls upset her.

On Friday of the same week he appeared in the *Guardian* newsroom. Jessica, who had caught sight of him near the bank of elevators, came over to Sara's desk to warn her that he was in the building. Sara had several colleagues in the newsroom who wouldn't mind it if the sharp-tongued, hip Cuban lieutenant was humbled and brought down a peg or two. Ever since the corruption charges, Alex had been using his whiplash sense of humor to castigate those responsible for Centac's crucifixion in the newspaper. Egos had been pricked. Now was the golden opportunity to retaliate. It was no secret that Sara and Alex had been a hot twosome. It was equally no secret that they were no longer together. When the macho lieutenant with the burning eyes strolled into the newsroom, antennae went up and eyeballs clicked, following him.

"There's someone over there who seems to want to see you. He doesn't look like he's here on official business, though," Michelle Langley drawled to Sara. Sara looked up from the contact sheets on her desk and blanched. She put down the loupe she was holding. Her heart clenched at the sight of Alex, but her soft mouth formed a resolute line. She'd thought he would leave. She should have known better.

"Would you tell him I don't want to see him? His memory isn't too good lately. He needs to be constantly reminded."

"My pleasure," Jack Paterson said with a leer.

She wanted Alex to know that he was fighting a losing battle trying to communicate with her. All her loyal friends in the newsroom had strict instructions to keep him at bay. She knew Alex wouldn't make a scene, for he was not one to wish to air his dirty linen in public. That night on the cruise had been an exception; Raphael had goaded him into aggression. She was a little surprised, therefore, when he kept on coming, even after Jack Paterson exchanged a few well-chosen words with him.

He strode up to her desk. In a low, heated voice, his eyes locked onto hers, he rapped his finger sharply on the desk. "You and I are going to talk, Sara. Make no mistake about it."

"Are we?" she said with wide-eyed wonder. "Whatever are we going to talk about with that chasm yawning between us?"

There were titters from a nearby desk. She knew she was walking dangerously close to the edge, treading on his innate dignity. But she was past caring. It wasn't only the Raphael Cruzeros of this world who behaved recklessly when they were hopping mad.

His eyes were a mirror of sharp-edged humor, intent desire and formidable willpower. Everything that was male about him emanated from him in waves—the dark flashing eyes, the dark good looks, the deep blue of the suit he wore. It was as if the banked fire between them intensified everything—colors, sights and sounds.

He darted a look over his shoulder, as he backed away. "You are going to regret this, Sara. Remember that."

She already *had,* she thought bitterly.

When he had disappeared into an elevator, some of the women in the newsroom swooned.

"If you don't want him, can we have him?" the woman feature writer who wrote the dance reviews whispered sotto voce, with the phone receiver tucked underneath her chin. She smiled wickedly.

Sara's eyes shot back to the bank of elevators. Her heart hardened again and her resolve returned when she remembered the calculating Don Juan role he had played. A woman had to harden her heart with a man like Alex. There was no other way, unless she wanted her feelings trampled on again and again. She guessed he would catch up with her sooner or later, but she would be better prepared when she was back on track. At the moment she still felt too vulnerable to cope with a meeting. She needed time to heal a broken heart. Besides, he hadn't suffered enough yet, she thought as she turned her attention to the contact sheets in front of her.

A few evenings later Alex sat in the Brasserie, one of the better steak houses in Miami, with two friends from the force. He never ate at home these days, he reflected. And he didn't have to remind himself why. The condo was cold and empty, and he hated going home to it; he stayed out with the men he worked with for as long as possible. One of the guys from the department was telling a story about how a rapist was bitten by one of his victims on a vital piece of his anatomy. He had to go for reconstructive surgery.

The laughter was dying down, when Alex's dark head swung sharply toward the door of the restaurant. He saw Sara walking in with a man. With a lowered gaze, as if he weren't watching them at all, he followed them as they made their way through the restaurant. The man at her side looked like an attorney he had seen in court. Or was he one of the editors from the newspaper she worked for? What difference did it make? Jealousy gnawed at his insides like some predatory animal. He didn't want anybody near her except him.

His gaze slid slowly over her. She was wearing a black suit that outlined her curves. Her hair was pulled back from her face, showing off the fine bone structure just below the velvet-smooth surface of her skin. When she saw him, her gray eyes flashed like molten silver. For a long telling moment they just looked at each other, then she turned her head abruptly.

But Alex couldn't take his eyes off her now, and he made no more effort to disguise his interest. He looked at the man next to her, wondering if he had put his hands on her. The thought of anyone else touching her nearly drove him out of his chair over to their table. Everything Latin in him wanted to go, but he told himself he had to cool down. If he wanted Sara back, making a public scene wasn't the way to get her. Their future together hung by a fine thread; if he charged in there now he could lose her forever.

So he waited, the green-eyed monster gnawing at his vitals. He consoled himself with the knowledge that for that moment when her eyes met his, something had flared between them. Deep satisfaction shot through him when he saw that look. She could tell herself she didn't want any part of him, she could pretend all she liked, but he knew she wanted the same thing he did. Before he had been the one lying to himself; now it was Sara. He recognized the look in her eyes; it was the same the first time he met her seven years ago. It was the same one he had seen the night he walked into the Polo Lounge. He watched her say something to her companion. It looked as if she was suggesting they go somewhere else. But her puzzled companion indicated with his hand the Reserved sign on the table, and she acquiesced. Alex watched in simmering silence as Sara sat down to have dinner with her friend. She acted as if he weren't there. But he knew she was as acutely aware of his presence as he was of hers.

In the week that followed he caught the occasional glimpse of her coming out of the courts with other members of the media. Once when he was out working he deliberately parked the car near a place she ate lunch, in hope of seeing her. Alex knew he would get his chance sooner or later, but the sexual tension mounted as the week crawled by.

Sara found it increasingly difficult to get through the workday. Not only was pregnancy making her queasy in the morning and overemotional, she was missing Alex a hundred times more than she admitted to herself. She tried burying him in the back of her mind as if he no longer existed. But Alex wasn't the kind of man who would play dead, not a hot-blooded Latin with formidable willpower. Besides, her own true feelings gave her away with monotonous regularity.

On a Monday morning she stepped out of the morgue into a corridor, feeling light-headed. There was a hunt on for a serial rapist. Another young woman had been brutally raped and beaten, then stabbed to death. Sara went with the reporter each time a new victim turned up. She and Herb Olsen had been to the scene of the homicide and had gone to the morgue to talk with the coroner. It had been a testing morning, Sara thought, as she leaned against the wall. Her legs felt rubbery, and she thought she was going to either faint or be sick—she wasn't sure which. Taking deep steadying breaths, she waited for Herb, an old hand hardened to gruesome details. He was still inside joking with the coroner. From here they had to go to another assignment.

She closed her eyes, waiting for the queasy sensation to pass. Finally she rummaged in her camera bag for some soda crackers she kept handy. Footsteps echoed down the corridor, coming her way. They slowed, then stopped a few feet away. She opened her eyes. Alex's charismatic face swam in front of her.

She groaned inwardly. Of all the times and places he had to catch up with her, fate would pick now. Not only did she feel absolutely miserable, she looked awful. Vanity, thy name is woman, she thought.

She tried to push out of his way, but he caught her arm. "What are you doing here?" she demanded. "Following me?"

"Drug-related homicide. But I knew I would run into you sooner or later."

"Stay away from me. I still feel like cutting your heart out," she pointed out. "Especially the way I feel this morning," she added.

"So you're not feeling so hot," he said.

He was pure macho, proud of what he had done. She looked to see if anyone was coming, but there was nobody in sight. She saw the possessive gleam, the amused, claiming look in his eyes, sizing her up as a pregnant and therefore vulnerable woman.

"Are you trying to blame me for how you feel?" he asked.

"You had something to do with it."

Her words only made him smile. "You can't blame your condition entirely on me," he murmured in a low intimate tone. "'Cause I remember you giving me a lot of help." His lazy humor set her flesh quivering. Her mind and her body ached for him every time she saw him. Only it made her absolutely miserable to admit it.

He knew it, and it strengthened his resolve and brought out everything protective about him. "How much longer are you going to be able to run around doing this job? Can't you cut it?"

"I'm still here," she pointed out with a speaking look, meaning her job with the newspaper. Meaning she hadn't run away from Miami, either.

The silence lengthened as they studied each other. It was two weeks since they broke up. Something clenched, then turned over deep inside her. She wanted to run from his overwhelming nearness, to escape from those eyes that saw everything and told her nothing. But he propped his hand alongside her head, fixing her with an expression of deceptive amiability.

"You know what they say—if you can't take the heat, you have to get out of the kitchen." His eyes darted to the swinging doors of the morgue she had just emerged from.

"There's only one kind of heat I can't take, and that's the kind you put out." Her feminine outrage resurfaced. She accused him silently of all that had happened in the few months since they had been reunited.

"In a few more months what are you going to do, Sara? About work?" He smiled at the picture that formed in his mind. She wanted to slap his face.

"I'll take a short leave of absence. I can do freelance work."

"Come on, Sara."

She started to move past him. "I'll think of something."

Something inside him softened. "I don't want you endangering my kid or yourself," he asserted quietly.

She looked at him, silenced by his words, experiencing a chilling sense of déjà vu. This was so familiar, so similar to, a scene that had played seven years ago.

"We've hardly made any progress at all. We're still the same people, a little bit older but sadly no wiser. We still have this huge communication gap yawning between us, and the only way you can think of to bridge it is by ordering me around. Is this where you start to tell me what we are and aren't going to do?"

Closing his eyes, as if he were marshaling his own deeper emotions, he responded, his hands clasped her shoulders. "No, Sara. That's not what I want to talk to you about. That's not what I've been wanting to tell you for these past weeks."

She watched him lower his gaze to gather his thoughts.

"We are not going to play that scene all over again. Believe me, this time is different." His eyes searched hers, pleading with her to believe what came next, that he was in earnest. "I love you, Sara. I don't think I ever stopped loving you. Maybe I told myself I did. All those years we were apart I had it in the back of my mind that you would come back, only I never admitted it to myself.

"When you finally did come back and I saw you with Cruzero, all I could think of was getting even. Seeing you again churned up all kinds of feelings inside me I didn't know I had. Raphael was sitting there beside you and I was already after him. I wanted him, he wanted you, I wanted you. I thought, why not? Why not milk the situation for all it was worth? It was as if it had been set up, designed exclusively for me to exploit. I told myself I'd be a fool to pass it up," he added quietly, "because I could see you still wanted me, too."

The low rhythmic intimacy of his hard-hitting words brought the sting of tears to her eyes.

"But that wasn't how it worked out. I was so hip, so sharp, I almost cut myself and bled to death." He laughed softly before he continued, his expression sober. "I almost lost you, Sara, before I woke up to what

I was doing. When I heard you talking on the telephone to your sister it really hit me. I want you to know no one has ever come close to making me feel the way you make me feel. While we were together these past months, those words that kept slipping out weren't part of any act, Sara. That was me telling you what I really felt. When I told you I had to see you again, that was no lie. What I told you that day at the airport about losing it when you turn your back on me, that was no line to get you to stay. I might have told myself that, but it was the truth. Don't turn your back on me now." His hands caught her face.

They were words he'd needed to say and she'd needed to hear. They shook her; they reached deep inside her to satisfy a yearning that had gone on for seven years, that had led her blindly back to Miami. Now they brought an inner peace that nothing else could.

Sara's eyes were filling with tears. His lips brushed hers with aching tenderness, and her lips responded, mating with his.

He lifted his head and continued. "Raphael wasn't the only one caught in a trap," he announced with a steady warm glow in his eyes. "You had me trapped from the first time I saw you. No contest there," he whispered kissing the end of her nose.

He concluded his impassioned plea. "Come back with me, Sara. It's where you belong, now more than ever."

Sara's lips moved against the side of his face telling him it was where she always wanted to be. He gathered her in his arms and murmured her name over and over, drawing her closer, kissing her again and again. People passed them in the hallway, but neither of them noticed. And when they broke apart to walk down the corridor together side by side, Alex curved his arm tightly around her shoulder. There was no gap of any kind between them now.

Epilogue

Sara heard the front door to the condo slam and she walked out of the kitchen to see Alex. A little boy making *vroom, vroom, vroom* noises followed her on his tricycle. Pausing and looking down at their son, she attempted to look stern. "Robert, I told you not to ride that in the house. Only outside."

Her gaze roamed over the six-foot frame of the man who had just walked in. After four and a half years of marriage, Alex was still a magnet. He shrugged out of his jacket and tossed it onto a nearby chair.

"What did your mother say about riding the bike in the house, shortstop?" Robert wore his favorite hat, a baseball cap given to him by his doting grandfather.

"Not to," the three-and-a-half-year-old said vibrantly, still sitting firmly on the saddle of the bike.

"You have to do what your mother says," Alex said firmly, but warmly.

Removing his gun and shoulder holster, then locking them safely away in a cabinet, Alex turned to the little boy who watched every move he made.

"C'mere, shortstop." The little boy got off the tricycle and ran into his father's arms. Sara leaned back against the doorway watching them with a smile on her face. It was Robert's greatest joy to be swung around by his father.

When Alex paused from their game and looked over at Sara she said, "You're early."

"I thought we might celebrate tonight."

She looked surprised: his birthday wasn't for another four days. Still, if he wanted to celebrate early, the weekend was really a better time to celebrate than the middle of the week. Today was Friday.

"I want to take the lady of my life out to dinner," he announced, turning on the charm and holding Robert high up in the air as the child laughed with delight.

"Why?" she queried as a slow smile invaded the corners of her mouth. They flirted with each other across the space of the living room until he walked over, still holding Robert in his arms and leaned down to answer her question.

"Because she told me last night that we are going to have a new addition to our family in several more months. Because I have a birthday to celebrate and because I happen to love her very much. Those are all very good reasons to celebrate. Maybe she wants to hear a few more," he whispered softly, the movement of his lips caressing the side of her face.

"I think she might take you up on your offer," she murmured back. His words and the warmth in his eyes made her want to kiss him, so she turned her head to meet his questing lips.

A small hand intervened. "Me first."

Alex turned his dark head sideways, regarding his small son with deepening amusement. "Okay, you first."

A small wet mouth pursued Sara's cheek until it reached its desired target.

"Is it all right if I kiss her now? I have your permission?" A smile split Alex's face as Robert bobbed his head up and down in agreement, then watched his father lean over to kiss his mother.

"Can you be ready in an hour—I have a table booked. What about shortstop, here?"

"I can call your mother, she's always willing to come over and baby-sit."

Loosening his tie with his free hand, he pulled it from around his neck, his fingers attacking the top buttons of his shirt while his other arm stayed firmly locked around their little boy.

"My bike is broken, Daddy."

"Is that why it's in the house? You want me to fix it?" Her husband's and son's voices faded into the background as Sara picked up the phone to call her mother-in-law.

Sometime later, Alex strode into the bedroom. She could hear the television on in the living room and knew that Robert would watch it until his grandmother arrived.

"I love you," Alex breathed against the side of her neck, pulling her into his arms again. The happy news that there was another child on the way affected them both deeply. Flushing with pleasure, she received another kiss before he moved away into their bathroom. In a few minutes the shower was running.

"Where are we going?" she called out over the sound of pelting water.

"I thought it would be nice if we went somewhere really classy. Why don't you wear that black dress?" he shouted back.

Which black dress? she wondered to herself, frowning at the contents of the wardrobe. Unsure of what he meant, she slipped on clean lingerie, then began brushing her hair. A few minutes later he came out, half-naked and wet with only a towel wrapped around his hips, his dark hair slicked back.

"Which black dress are you talking about?"

"The black lace one. It goes like this," he said, and she watched him make some comical gestures with his hands, indicating the neckline with typical male vagueness about such things. She stared at him perplexed, then walked slowly over to the wardrobe.

Riffling through the dresses, she reached to the very back of the closet where she put things she hadn't worn for years. "You mean this," she inquired, pulling out a two piece outfit. The black lace top had a sweetheart neckline, a wide black satin belt and a slim matching skirt.

He stared at it as he dried his hair with a towel. "Yeah, that's the one."

She regarded the dress thoughtfully for a moment, then something clicked in her mind.

"Where did you say we were going? I hope it's somewhere very dressy because I'm going to look out of place in this outfit if it isn't."

"I thought someplace like the Polo Lounge would be nice," he said with a broad grin. Coming up behind her, Alex locked his arms around her waist. She knew Alex very well by now; he never did anything without a specific purpose in mind. All she had to do was figure out what it was, and she always did. As his hands locked on her hips and he drew her back into the solid warmth of his body, his lips explored the side of her neck.

"What do you want for your birthday? You still haven't told me." She had asked him a few days ago but he had been noncommittal.

"A kiss. Right in the middle of the Polo Lounge," he teased softly. "What do you think about that?"

She leaned back and closed her eyes, laughing deep in her throat and thinking she had everything a woman could want—a man who loved her, a child she adored and another on the way, a job she enjoyed, and a settled way of life. But Alex still liked to remind her from time to time that he would still always *try* to get his own way. That's the way it would always be, and she really didn't have any argument with that.

*   *   *   *   *

For all those readers who've been looking for something a little bit different, a little bit spooky, let Silhouette Books take you on a journey to the dark side of love with

SILHOUETTE
Shadows™

If you like your romance mixed with a hint of danger, a taste of something eerie and wild, you'll love Shadows. This new line will send a shiver down your spine and make your heart beat faster. It's full of romance and more—and some of your favorite authors will be featured right from the start. Look for our four launch titles wherever books are sold, because you won't want to miss a single one.

THE LAST CAVALIER—Heather Graham Pozzessere
WHO IS DEBORAH?—Elise Title
STRANGER IN THE MIST—Lee Karr
SWAMP SECRETS—Carla Cassidy

After that, look for two books every month, and prepare to tremble with fear—and passion.

SILHOUETTE SHADOWS, coming your way in March.

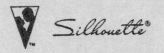

Silhouette®

SHAD1

AMERICAN HERO

It seems readers can't get enough of these men—and we don't blame them! When Silhouette Intimate Moments' best authors go all-out to create irresistible men, it's no wonder women everywhere are falling in love. And look what—and who!—we have in store for you early in 1993.

January brings NO RETREAT (IM #469), by Marilyn Pappano. Here's a military man who brings a whole new meaning to macho!

In February, look for IN A STRANGER'S EYES (IM #475), by Doreen Roberts. Who is he—and why does she feel she knows him?

In March, it's FIREBRAND (IM #481), by Paula Detmer Riggs. The flames of passion have never burned this hot before!

And in April, look for COLD, COLD HEART (IM #487), by Ann Williams. It takes a mother in distress and a missing child to thaw this guy, but once he melts...!

AMERICAN HEROES. YOU WON'T WANT TO MISS A SINGLE ONE—ONLY FROM

IMHERO3R

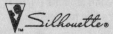

It takes a very special man to win

She's friend, wife, mother—she's you! And beside each Special Woman stands a wonderfully *special* man. It's a celebration of our heroines—and the men who become part of their lives.

Look for these exciting titles from Silhouette Special Edition:

January **BUILDING DREAMS** by Ginna Gray

February **HASTY WEDDING** by Debbie Macomber

March **THE AWAKENING** by Patricia Coughlin

April **FALLING FOR RACHEL** by Nora Roberts

Dont miss THAT SPECIAL WOMAN! each month—from your special authors.

AND

For the most special woman of all—you, our loyal reader—we have a wonderful gift: a beautiful journal to record all of your special moments. See this month's THAT SPECIAL WOMAN! title for details.

TSW1

NORA ROBERTS

Love has a language all its own, and for centuries flowers have symbolized love's finest expression. Discover the language of flowers—and love—in this romantic collection of 48 favorite books by bestselling author Nora Roberts.

Two titles are available each month at your favorite retail outlet.

In January, look for:

Summer Desserts, Volume #23
This Magic Moment, Volume #24

In February, look for:

Lessons Learned, Volume #25
The Right Path, Volume #26

Collect all 48 titles
and become fluent in
THE LANGUAGE of LOVE

Silhouette®

**Silhouette Intimate Moments
is proud to present
Mary Anne Wilson's
SISTER, SISTER duet—
Two halves of a whole,
two parts of a soul**

In the mirror, Alicia and Alison Sullivan both had
brilliant red hair and green eyes—but in
personality and life-style, these identical twins
were as different as night and day. Alison
needed control, order and stability. Alicia, on
the other hand, hated constraints, and the idea
of settling down bored her.

Despite their differences, they had one thing in
common—a need to be loved and cherished by
a special man. And to fulfill their goals, these
two sisters would do anything for each other—
including switching places in a life-threatening
situation.

Look for Alison and Jack's adventure in TWO FOR
THE ROAD (IM #472, January 1993), and Alicia
and Steven's story in TWO AGAINST THE WORLD
(IM #489, April 1993)—and *enjoy!*

SISTERR

INTIMATE MOMENTS®
™ *Silhouette* ®